A LIZ ADAMS MYSTERY

A Camping Conundrum

STACY WILDER

Cover design by Brandi Doane McCann

ISBN: 979-8-9907831-2-6 (paperback)

ISBN: 979-8-9907831-3-3 (hardback)

ISBN: 979-8-9907831-4-0 (ebook)

www.storystacy.com

Chapter 1

I gazed into my vanity table's beveled glass mirror and swept a coat of mascara onto my lashes. The reflection of our plush, king-sized comforter made me question my sanity. How had my husband convinced me to sleep on the ground in a tent in just ten days from today? The thought of the possible creepy crawlies that might join us in the small space caused me to shudder.

As I placed the wand back into the tube, a terrifying memory of a Girl Scout camping trip rushed forth from the depths of my mind. The container tumbled out of my hands and onto the table, leaving an ebony splotch on the white surface. I ignored the mess while the vivid recollection played out.

My favorite Girl Scout counselor navigated the highway that led to the campground outside of Atlanta where we'd pitch our tents. Inside the van, the mood was festive, and I couldn't wait to add the coveted camping badge to my collection of awards. The noise level escalated as the rowdy group of ten-year-olds chatted about our latest crushes and favorite TV shows. Our chaperones told us to keep the racket down several times.

After we arrived, we unloaded the camping gear, and the counselors demonstrated how to set up our tents. My friend and I wrestled with the poles for half an hour before we claimed victory. By dinner time, I was starving. Our troop collected logs, built a fire, and roasted a feast of hot dogs, baked beans, and corn on the cob. As a magical golden full moon rose, we sang songs and toasted marshmallows over the flames. I licked the melted chocolate that oozed out the side of a s'more, and my taste-buds tingled.

When it was time to clean up, clouds drifted overhead, and the sky darkened. Two men with pantyhose over their heads appeared out of nowhere. I trembled at the sight of their mushed faces. While they waved knives at the counselors, the men demanded money and food. The adults motioned for us to sit on nearby logs while they emptied their wallets into a paper sack. Several girls screamed, and the men shouted at us to shut up. My heart pounded in my chest. I clamped my hands over my ears and squeezed my eyes shut. When my friend nudged me and whispered, "They're gone," I lowered my shaking palms.

The adults called the cops and then ushered us into the van, where we huddled together until the police arrived. The sound of sobs filled the space, and I couldn't stop shaking. We never completed the trip, so I never earned that badge—and I never went camping again.

While I wiped away the splotch on the vanity with a tissue, I wished that I could erase the memory from my mind as easily.

Earlier, while Brad and I sat at the kitchen table eating breakfast, he'd brought up the idea. "What do you think about taking a long weekend camping trip? I know just the spot."

I'd responded with a firm no. His crestfallen look caused me to reconsider. When he'd shared fond memories of his family trips to Poinsett Park, South Carolina, my resolve crumbled.

Brad lost both his sister and his parents to separate tragic acci-dents. His ten-year-old sister drowned, and his parents perished on Flight 93 on 9/11. Who was I to deprive him of reliving his cherished childhood experiences?

His stories tugged on my heartstrings, and before I knew it, I'd changed my answer to yes. Brad hustled toward his laptop to book the trip, leaving behind a half-eaten plate of scrambled eggs.

After my sudden recollection, I wondered if I should reconsider. He'd understand my reluctance once I shared my Girl Scout horror story. I hesitated, then decided to keep the memory to myself. No reason to spoil his excitement about our upcoming adventure. If I felt too vulnerable in the tent, I could always take refuge in the Sprinter van that Brad had gifted me as a wedding present last year.

I sighed with resignation, then rose from my vanity table to exchange my robe for a black camisole and jeans. Once a month, the women in our neighborhood gathered for an evening of fun and friendly competition. Tonight, my next-door neighbor, Maria, was hosting a karaoke contest combined with a *cabi* clothing event. One of her coworkers, Michelle, recently left the shipping company where they both worked to become a full-time *cabi* stylist, and Maria was supporting her new venture.

I'd deliberately chosen my outfit so I could easily try on the merchandise. Since the early May temperatures were cool, I added a black lace shrug. A pair of cream-colored espadrilles completed the ensemble. I spritzed my neck with my favorite perfume, Amazing Grace.

When I entered the living room, Brad and our black Lab, Duke, were settled on the couch watching a baseball game. The doorbell rang, and our dog made a beeline for the door.

"I'll get it." I held Duke's collar and exchanged fresh, warm pizza for the cash Brad had left on the front table. Duke's tail swished at the smell of garlic and pepperoni. After I placed the box on the kitchen counter, I grabbed the bouquet of flowers I'd bought for Maria, kissed Brad goodbye, and headed next door.

***

"Liz, come in." Maria accepted the bunch of parrot tulips in varying shades of orange and pink. "Thank you. You didn't need to do this."

"You're welcome," I said.

She motioned ahead. "Everyone's in the kitchen."

While Maria placed the bouquet in a crystal vase, I joined the women gathered around the center island. White platters and bowls with spring rolls, egg rolls, Chinese chicken salad, wontons, and various sauces created an eye-appealing spread across the mushroom-gray granite countertop.

I listened in silence while everyone chatted. The camping memory still lingered at the back of my mind, and I hoped that I could shake my sense of unease and enjoy the camaraderie.

"Everything OK, Liz?" my neighbor, Linda, asked.

She must have noticed my somber mood. "Yeah. I'm alright. It's just..." I hesitated. "I let Brad talk me into a camping trip, and then I remembered a bad experience I had as a kid. Kinda shook me up."

Linda cocked her head. "You? Camping?"

"Guess I don't come across as the outdoorsy type?" I laughed.

"I'll say." She patted my shoulder. "So, what happened, Sweetie?"

"Not now. I'll tell you later."

"I know what you need." Linda grabbed a stemless wine glass from the opposing countertop and poured a generous glass of sauvignon blanc.

I accepted the beverage and swallowed a large gulp. "Thanks."

"You're welcome. Drink up." She changed the subject. "What are you going to sing tonight?"

"Haven't decided yet. How about you?" I set my glass down, placed an egg roll on a rectangular plate, and added a spoonful of hot mustard.

"'O Canada.' I hope it's on the song menu." Linda winked.

Since she was originally from there, I was confident she knew the tune by heart.

"Everyone, please load up your plates and grab a seat in the living room. Michelle is ready to get started," Maria announced.

I added chicken salad with crunchy noodles and mandarin oranges to my plate and then topped off my sauvignon blanc.

A long rack of clothes blocked the view of the brick fireplace. Maria had lined up her wooden dining chairs in front of the display. Once everyone was seated, Michelle introduced herself. "Good evening, ladies. I'm Michelle, a stylist with *cabi*. I love my new job, and tonight we are going to have some fun."

She passed out pens, forms, and catalogs with descriptions of each item. "*Cabi* helps women in need around the world." She expounded on the statistics of the women the company had aided with the proceeds from the clothing sales. "If you round up your purchases, the donations will help us make a difference."

Michelle held up an example of the form where we could record our preferences. "Mark what you like as I show you the clothing line. There will be time to try on your selections afterward, and I'm happy to answer any questions about sizes. Please tell me your names. I already know Maria. Let's start with you." She gestured toward Linda.

After we introduced ourselves to Michelle, she asked, "Does anyone have any upcoming travel plans?"

I groaned. "I'm going camping in ten days." My sixty-two-year-old neighbor, Cassie, gave me a puzzled look. I guess I had *not the outdoorsy type* stamped on my forehead. "Brad talked me into it," I explained.

Michelle clapped her hands. "Oh, I have the perfect clothing collection for that! I was going to start with Spring Luxe, but I'll start with Summer Fun instead. Get your pen ready, Liz."

As Michelle showcased items from each section of the catalog, she pointed out trends and different pieces that paired well together. After I tried on my choices in Maria's spare bedroom, I ended up purchasing four T-shirts, a skort, two pairs of shorts, and a windbreaker. I couldn't resist throwing in a pair of spiral silver earrings.

Michelle added up my total and assured me that the order would arrive in time for my upcoming trip.

Once everyone had completed their purchases, Michelle wheeled the rack of clothes into the entryway, and Maria herded us back to our seats. Our hostess slid an end table in front of the taupe brick fireplace and placed a karaoke machine on top of the surface.

Maria tapped the mic and then explained the rules. "Let's get ready to rumble! We'll start out as two teams and then progress to an individual competition. Liz, Cassie, and I will be Team One. Michelle, Gwen, and Linda, you'll be Team Two."

She cleared her throat and continued. "For the first round, each person will sing one song. Then each team will choose one person to eliminate. Any questions so far?"

Maria passed out the menu of preselected choices. I caught a frown on Linda's face and then noticed that "O Canada" wasn't listed.

No one had questions, so Maria continued. "After a second song, each team will pick the singer from their group who will move on to the final round. Once that round is complete, everyone will vote on the winner." She held up the prizes in her free hand. "The champion will get a fifty-dollar Visa gift card. Second place will receive a twenty-five-dollar gift card. Someone from Team One will sing first, followed by someone from Team Two. Ladies, let's get started!"

Since we'd all had a few glasses of wine, this was going to be fun.

"Liz, you're up." Maria handed me the microphone and cued up my song choice. As I watched the lyrics flash across the screen, I crooned B-52s' "Love Shack." Not an easy song with both the male and female parts, but I thought I nailed it.

My quiet librarian neighbor from Team Two, Gwen, followed. She shocked the crowd with a rendition of "These Boots Are Made for Walkin'" by Nancy Sinatra.

Dang. Gwen was in it to win it.

When everyone finished, each team made their picks, and Linda and Maria were eliminated.

Michelle started round two with "Crazy" by Patsy Cline. I botched Pat Benatar's "Hit Me with Your Best Shot." Cassie ended with a pitch-perfect "I Will Survive" by Gloria Gaynor. Michelle and I were eliminated.

Maria called a break before the championship session between Cassie and Gwen began.

We all whooped and hollered as the final round started.

Cassie took the mic first and belted out "The Lady Is a Tramp" by Ella Fitzgerald. She sashayed as she sang. Since her nickname was Sassy Cassie, it was the perfect song. Gwen followed with a mesmerizing performance of Julie Andrews' "My Favorite Things." Gwen won hands down.

It was past midnight when Linda and I walked home.

Linda nudged my arm. "So, tell me about your bad experience, Luv."

As I shared my horror story, she gasped. "How awful. And you never told Brad?"

"Honestly, I think I repressed the memory. The mention of camping brought it back."

"You need to tell him, Liz."

"No can do. He's so excited about going. I don't want him to cancel the trip. I've already committed. Anyway, my bad experience happened a long time ago. I'll be fine."

"Up to you. I'm here for you if you need anything." She hugged me.

"Thanks."

I unlocked the door, waved goodbye to Linda, and then stumbled into my house with a much better attitude about our getaway. After all, I was a kick-butt private investigator and not a ten-year-old child. I had my girlfriends to reach out to for support. I'd be there with my wonderful husband and our amazing dog. We'd have the Sprinter van, and I'd be dressed to the nines.

What could possibly go wrong?

Chapter 2

For the first day of our trip, I'd paired a *cabi* fuchsia-and-black striped tee with my new pair of black skorts. Before we left Charleston, we'd stocked the van's fridge and a large cooler with steaks, shrimp, marinated chicken kabobs, my favorite macaroni salad, dairy products, water, wine, beer, and an array of fruits and vegetables. I'd also loaded the cupboards with coffee, tea, and a smorgasbord of snacks, including ingredients for s'mores. A stack of books awaited in the console for my reading pleasure. Surely, I could survive a four-day camping trip.

As Brad drove the Sprinter down the highway leading to the campground, we listened to country tunes on the radio. Finally, a brown wooden sign with white lettering indicated that we had arrived at the entrance of Poinsett Park. Brad turned right onto a road lined with pine trees and followed the markers that pointed toward the park ranger station. Duke hung his head out the window of the Sprinter and inhaled the unfamiliar smells.

Brad grinned. "Everything looks just like I remembered."

He parked the vehicle in front, and I fastened the leash to Duke's collar. After our dog relieved himself on the front lawn, we entered the building. Duke's nails clicked against the polished pine floors, the sound echoing in the cozy space. Distressed pine walls exuded an old-fashioned charm. In the center of the room, a rack of metal shelves held souvenirs available for purchase.

A large man, dressed in a gunmetal-gray shirt and army-green pants, greeted us. "Welcome to Poinsett Park." He had a white walrus mustache that curled up at the ends, and his belly bulged over his brown leather belt. "I'm Park Ranger Pete. Been here over thirty-two years." His chest swelled with pride, and he extended his palm. He shook Brad's hand and then mine and patted Duke on the head. "Nice dog. How can I help you folks?" He had a deep voice that reverberated throughout the small space.

"That's Duke. I'm Brad, and this is Liz. We're checking in." Brad handed him a piece of paper with our name and reservation number.

"Right this way." Pete motioned toward the counter, checked a notebook, and confirmed the booking. He slid a bowl of Hershey Kisses my way. "Help yourself."

"Thanks." I reached into the dish, peeled the silver foil off the chocolate, and popped the candy into my mouth.

Pete handed Brad the paperwork. "Just a few forms for you to sign and then you can be on your way." While Brad filled out the information, Pete went over the park rules. "You'll need to keep your pet on a leash. Officially, there's a no-alcohol policy, but if you keep it in containers and don't cause any trouble, I don't have a problem with it. You folks don't look like troublemakers to me." He grabbed a map and a yellow highlighter and circled the spot where we'd hook up the van and pitch our tent. "You're in luck. We've had a few cancellations, and you won't have anyone on either side of you." He cleared his throat. "I need to warn you that we've had a few recent thefts."

"Thefts?" My stomach did a flip-flop. I fought the urge to hightail it out of there and reminded myself I was here for Brad.

"I'm sure it's just kids, and no one's been hurt. I'd keep any valuables out of sight and locked up inside of your van. Of course, your dog's also a deterrent."

"What's been stolen?" Brad asked.

"Bikes, cash, kayaks, liquor. Anything left out in the open or in an unlocked vehicle."

I'd checked before we left. The park had an open carry policy, and I breathed a sigh of relief that I'd brought my gun. In my line of work, I rarely left home without it.

Pete continued, "The thieves tend to strike after dark and are dressed in hoodies with bandanas over their faces. According to witnesses, there are three of them. We recently installed additional cameras around the campsites. It's only a matter of time until they're caught." He gave each of us a business card with a handwritten number on the back. "That's my personal cell. If you see anything suspicious, feel free to call me."

He ushered us out the front door and pointed toward the road we needed to follow to reach our site. "Let me know if there's anything else I can do for you folks. Enjoy your stay."

Branches crunched underneath the tires as our van bumped down the narrow dirt road. On our way out, Pete handed us a folder filled with tourist information. I opened the packet and studied the enclosed map. To the southeast, a lake bordered the ranger station. Trails wound throughout the park. Small squares with numbers indicated the location of campsites and cabins. A back entrance led toward the rangers' residences.

While I read through a visitor guide for the nearby town of Sumter, I turned toward Brad and said, "Maybe we should stay at the Hampton Inn in Sumter." I'd already checked their policy on pets. They allowed dogs. If my nerves got the better of me, the hotel was a solid backup plan.

I added, "We can explore the park during the day and spend our nights at the Hampton."

Brad glanced my way with a confused look on his face. "Why? We're already here."

"Didn't you hear Pete say there were thefts at night?"

"Since when do you shy away from thieves?"

I briefly considered sharing the story of my Girl Scout trip and then bit my tongue. I sighed and reminded myself once again that I was an experienced PI, not a kid, and that I was here for my husband.

"You're right. I normally don't. I just thought it'd be better to avoid the drama." Our last trip had been filled with chaos. "Of course, if you'd rather stay, I'm good with that."

Duke yipped. Someone once told me that all dogs have superpowers. Duke's superpower was communication. He whined when something was up. He yipped when someone wasn't telling the truth. Very few people knew of his abilities. Of course, Brad was one of them.

"Liar," he laughed. "I tell you what. Once we're parked at the campsite, why don't you take Duke for a walk on one of the trails? I promise you're going to love this place. When you get back, I'll have lunch ready. After we eat, if you still want to leave, we'll go."

My heart swelled with gratitude at Brad's willingness to stay in town. "OK."

"I recommend walking the Coquina Trail. It's a shorter trek that leads to the waterfall."

Brad parked the van, and I pulled my blonde ponytail through the back of a baseball cap before sliding on a pair of sunglasses. Pine trees overshadowed our campsite, and we had a distant view of the lake. While Brad placed plates and utensils on the wooden picnic table, Duke and I wandered along the path that led to the waterfall. Clouds drifted overhead, and rays of sunlight streamed through the soft, billowy shapes.

The temperature hovered in the mid-seventies, and a soft breeze blew from the north. Duke sniffed the ground and paused when he smelled something of interest. Along the trail, olive-green moss draped over gnarled branches. Fuchsia, lilac, and white azalea bushes bloomed on either side of the path. A pair of male and female cardinals flitted between pine tree branches and chirped, "cheer, cheer." I inhaled a deep breath of fresh air and savored the earthy smells.

The sound of gushing water reached my ears long before we discovered the sight. I slapped at a mosquito and wished that I'd remembered to spritz both of us with the citronella bug spray I'd bought for the trip. When we arrived at the spillway, I perched on a tree stump and admired the view. Duke obediently sat by my side. Water tumbled down multi-levels of wood-framed tiers. Coquina bricks and rocks splotched with lime-green lichen bordered the cascading stream.

A ping from my phone interrupted the serene scene.

Linda: How's the camping?

I could hear her Canadian lilt through the words.

Me: It's OK.

I started to tell her about the thieves then erased the words. Too much information and emotion to squeeze into a text.

Linda liked my comment and then added: Don't be surprised if you hear from the girls. I didn't share what you told me. I only said that you might need some support from us.

Me: Thanks for the heads-up.

I set the phone down and returned to the landscape in front of me. Frogs croaked while a red-tailed hawk dove into the water and then surfaced with a small fish. Duke spied a squirrel and tugged on his leash. The sights and sounds soothed my senses, and the tension slowly evaporated from my limbs.

A ruby-throated hummingbird—Peg's favorite bird—whizzed by and then hovered in front of me. My breath caught. Next month would mark the two-year anniversary of my best friend Peg's death. I placed my hand over my heart as the tiny creature darted away. Was it a sign? A nudge from Peg urging me to stay strong?

I could do this. For Brad. For me. For us.

Park Ranger Pete said the thieves were just kids. I had a gun. I had our dog. I had Brad. With renewed resolve, I strode back toward the campsite.

When I spotted the colorful spread of food laid out on the table, I stopped and stared. Macaroni salad, a charcuterie board, and a fresh green salad adorned the surface. My mouth watered, and my stomach grumbled at the sight.

Brad poured sun tea from a jar into a plastic cup of ice and handed the beverage to me. "What'd you decide?"

"I'm good with staying."

"You're sure?"

"Yeah. Even if the thieves try to rob us, what harm can they do? We can keep anything of value locked up in the van." My insides flip-flopped, and I took a long sip of the cool drink to settle my nerves. "The trail was nice, and I found some hammocks where I can lounge and read while you train for the race."

Brad's triathlon was next month in Colorado, and we'd scheduled a road trip with friends for the occasion. While we were here, he'd take advantage of the trails and the lake to prepare for the competition.

"Great. It's settled. After lunch, I'll set up the tent and hook up the van." He placed a bowl of water on the ground for Duke. As our dog lapped up the liquid, Brad piled macaroni salad onto the blue-and-white melamine plates and then surprised me with a lobster claw salad. The guy knew my love language. Some girls wanted diamonds. I craved lobster. Duke thumped his tail and begged for crumbs.

After our meal, I stood and stretched. "I think I'll get comfy in a hammock while you pitch the tent."

Brad pulled me into a hug and kissed me in that toe-tingling way that left me breathless. For a fleeting moment, I felt excited about sleeping outside on the hard ground with my husband curled up next to me. He stepped back and grinned. "When I'm done setting up, I'm going on a bike ride."

Once I'd settled into a sling stretched between two oak trees, I opened my paperback copy of Julie Mulhern's latest cozy mystery. Duke nestled in a shaded patch of grass. He didn't care for being tethered, but rules were rules. The breeze washed over me as I turned the pages. Despite the compelling plot, my eyes closed, and sleep overcame me.

Brad interrupted my slumber when he leaned over and kissed my cheek. He whispered in my ear, "Hey, sleepy."

My eyes fluttered open.

"Why don't I take a shower and then start the fire for dinner? Care to join me?"

My heart leapt at the suggestion. "Absolutely."

I was grateful for the Sprinter van with a full bathroom, which meant that we didn't have to use the community restrooms. Although they were probably clean, I wasn't taking any chances. I glanced at my watch—four o'clock.

The space was barely big enough for the two of us, but we managed to make love behind closed doors while Duke lounged on the floor of the air-conditioned vehicle.

Afterward, we gathered dinner supplies and carted them outside. Brad lit the starter twigs in the fire pit for the steaks. I looped Duke's leash around a sturdy log, settled into a lawn chair, and queued up some songs on my phone. "The House of the Rising Sun" streamed first, followed by Johnny Cash's "Ring of Fire."

The flames crackled, and Brad added the meat to the grill. While I hummed to the music, the scent of garlic-seasoned tenderloins wafted within the smoke. Brad added foil packets of bacon-wrapped asparagus to the surface, and my mouth watered. Duke's nose wiggled, and his tail swept the ground in anticipation of the feast.

Twinkling stars and a crescent moon appeared in the sky as the temperature dropped to the mid-sixties. I uncorked the wine bottle and poured each of us a generous glass of cabernet into plastic cups. "Tell me about your camping trips with your family."

Brad's expression grew pensive as he sipped his wine in the chair next to me. "We'd typically head to the park on a Thursday and spend the weekend here. My dad worked hard, but when we camped, he didn't seem to have a care in the world. He and I would fish at the lake and then clean the catch for Mom to grill." He closed his eyes as he recalled the memories. "While we were gone, my mom and my sister would hang out at the campsite, reading or playing games. Before dinner, we'd all take a long walk, and then after our meal, we'd sit around the campfire and sing."

"What kind of songs?"

He chuckled. "Usually "The Wheels on the Bus" and then "Brown Eyed Girl" for my little sister. She had these chocolate eyes that you could get lost in." His voice softened. "Kristin's birthday is next month. She'd be thirty-five, and if she'd survived, she would've been beautiful." He wiped a stray tear from his cheek. "After she died, we came back, but it was never the same."

Kristen had drowned in their pool when Brad was thirteen—a tragedy that still haunted him. I reached over and squeezed his hand and then chastised myself for my selfishness. He deserved to relive these fond memories.

Brad asked, "What about your family? Did you guys ever go camping?"

I laughed. "Babs, camping?"

"Right. Dumb question. Although, I bet your dad likes to camp."

I was the only child of Barb—otherwise known as Babs to those closest to her—and Grant. "And don't get any big ideas in that head of yours about planning a camping trip with my parents." For a moment, I considered sharing my Girl Scout camping trip. When Brad stood to check on the steaks, I let the thought pass.

Once the meat was done, Brad loaded our plates and reserved a few bites for Duke. After dinner, we roasted s'mores over the fire. As the embers dwindled, I stifled a big yawn.

"Tired?"

"A little."

"Why don't you make yourself comfortable in the tent, and I'll clean up?"

Inwardly, I groaned. "Maybe we should sleep in the van. What about the thieves?"

"Don't worry." He kissed my cheek. "There's nothing better than sleeping outside under the stars. You'll love it. Just be sure to zip up the tent once you're inside."

"Why?"

"It's the best way to keep the roaches and other unwanted creatures out."

Since my husband had an intense fear of the insects, I nodded my assent. "Are you sure you don't need any help?" I gestured toward the dirty plates.

"Yep. You'll get KP tomorrow."

"KP?"

"Kitchen patrol. By the end of the weekend, you'll be a camping pro."

That'll be the day, I thought to myself as I unzipped the front of the four-person, mosquito-proof tent. A citronella diffuser emitted a citrus scent as an extra precaution against bugs. When I spotted the queen-sized air mattress, I smiled. Guess I wouldn't be sleeping on hard ground after all. There was plenty of room inside the tent for the two of us and Duke. I shed my clothes for my favorite sleepshirt and then slipped into the lightweight cotton sleeping bag.

As I nodded off, something slithery traveled over my leg, and I screamed, "Help!" I flew out of the bag and out of the unzipped tent.

Brad and Duke rushed to the tent. "What's the matter?"

"There's something slimy in our sleeping bag!"

Brad grabbed the sleep sack and dumped it upside down outside our tent. "A garter snake. Harmless, but I can understand why it spooked you."

The creature slithered away, and I had to restrain Duke from chasing the reptile.

"I don't do creepy crawlies. I'm sleeping in the Sprinter." I gave Brad a peck on the cheek and turned toward the van. "C'mon, Duke."

Our dog started to follow me and then changed his mind and trotted back to Brad. As I opened the van door, I prayed there wouldn't be any more unwanted surprises on this trip.

Chapter 3

Brad cradled a steaming cup of coffee while I sipped my hot tea. The mist from our mugs spiraled into the early morning fog. We turned our chairs for a view of the rising sun.

"How'd you sleep?" he asked.

"OK... once my heart rate recovered from that slimy snake." I adjusted the flannel blanket draped over my legs to ward off the chill in the air. "How about you?"

"I missed you, but I slept great. This guy slept like a log." He patted Duke's head. "Didn't you, boy?"

Duke thumped his tail in response.

I glanced sideways at Brad. The unspoken question of where I'd bunk tonight hung between us. "So, what's on the agenda for today?"

"After breakfast, why don't we take a bike ride? Then we can drive into Sumter for lunch."

"Perfect." I grinned. Although we'd only been here a day, I longed to get out of the woods and experience civilization.

Pete drove up in a golf cart, parked the vehicle, and approached us. We both stood to greet him.

"Morning, campers. How's your stay?"

"So far, so good other than the garter snake in the sleeping bag last night," I replied.

Pete chuckled. "You know they're harmless, right?"

I rolled my eyes. "Yeah, but that doesn't mean I have to sleep with them."

He smirked at Brad. "Guess she'll be glad we relocated the gators."

"Gators?" I gasped, wrapping the blanket tighter around me. Duke whined.

"Don't worry. *Those* reptiles are long gone. But... " His expression turned somber. "I do have some bad news. We had another theft last night."

My stomach dropped. "What kind of theft?"

Pete tugged on one side of his mustache, making his walrus tusks look lopsided. "Two dirt bikes disappeared from a campsite a few rows over." He pointed toward the east. "No need for concern—I'm on it."

"Thanks for letting us know," Brad said before Pete took off.

While the golf cart faded out of sight, I pleaded, "Can we please just leave?" My voice cracked in desperation.

He frowned, his forehead etched with worry. "Liz, what's up? I've never seen you this rattled."

The resurfaced memory broke through the wall I'd built around it. I could no longer hold back what happened on my Girl Scout camping trip. The words came rushing forth.

When I finished, Brad wrapped his arms around me. "I'm so sorry. Of course we can leave," he murmured in my ear. "Why didn't you tell me?"

"I thought I could handle it, and I didn't want to spoil the trip." Duke whimpered and nudged my leg. "It's alright, boy."

Ugh—so much for being a kick-butt private investigator and a wife who was empathetic to her husband's losses.

"That must've been awful. I had no idea." Brad rubbed my back, and the tension in my muscles eased. "Liz, don't keep something like that from me again."

"Alright." I sighed and then placed my head on his chest. The sound of his heartbeat soothed my nerves.

After a few minutes, he pulled away. "Let's pack our stuff. We can let Pete know why we're cutting our trip short on the way out."

I hesitated and drew a deep breath. A spark of my earlier resolve rekindled. What I'd been through paled in comparison to the trauma Brad experienced during his childhood. "Let's give it a day."

He gazed into my eyes. "Are you sure?"

I nodded. "Why don't we take that bike ride and search for clues?"

"That's my favorite PI." He grinned, and the worry lines on his forehead receded.

***

As soon as I retrieved the special bungee leash and no-pull harness from the van, Duke barked, danced in circles, and howled an "I love you." Our dog adored bike rides. We'd elected to leave the special cargo bike that I'd given Brad last Christmas back home. It was too bulky. Instead of riding in the large upfront basket, Duke would trot alongside our mountain bikes.

I sported my new *cabi* aquamarine sleeveless tee and knee-length black shorts. Although I still felt off balance after the news of the theft, the outfit bolstered my spirits. The sun blazed bright in a clear-blue, cloudless sky, and the temperature felt warmer than yesterday. I handed the leash to Brad, we mounted our bikes and then pedaled down the road toward the east, where Pete had pointed earlier. Duke pranced next to Brad's bike.

Up ahead, I spotted a couple, who looked to be in their fifties, seated in matching Atlanta Falcons folding chairs. While the man worked a crossword puzzle, the woman appeared to be knitting booties.

"Hey, neighbors." I waved as we approached. Brad and I parked our rides and dismounted.

The couple stood. "What a beautiful dog," the woman said. "May I pet him?"

"Of course. His name is Duke. I'm Liz, and this is my husband, Brad. We're just a few campsites down from you."

"I'm Clem, and this is Debbie." Our dog swished his tail in delight while Debbie massaged his neck. "Where you folks from?"

"Charleston," Brad said.

"We're from outside Atlanta. Visiting our nephew and his wife. They're stationed at Shaw Air Force Base," Debbie said.

As if on cue, a roar reverberated through the air, and three fighter jets flew overhead in a perfect vee formation.

We all shook hands before Debbie continued. "Our niece, Tracy, is due any day." She gestured toward the knitting project in progress. "It's a girl." A smile spread across her face.

"Congratulations," I said. "Have you heard anything about a theft last night?"

Debbie frowned. Clem kicked the ground with his foot. "That was us. Damn it. Those were four-thousand-dollar bikes. Of course they were insured, but what a hassle."

"Do you know what happened?" I asked.

Debbie shook her head. "Both of us wear noise-canceling sleep masks at night. Never heard a thing. When we woke up, the bikes were gone. We immediately went to the station to report it."

"Maybe I can help. I'm a PI in Charleston. Do you mind if our dog sniffs around? He has a great nose, and he might find something that Pete missed."

"Please do," Debbie said. "It'd be so much better if we could get our bikes back. I dread filling out paperwork and waiting on the insurance company." She pointed at Duke. "Is he a full-blooded Labrador retriever?"

"He is." In addition to Duke's lie-detecting ability, he had an amazing nose. If there was a clue to be found, I was confident that he'd discover it.

"Go find," I whispered the command in his ear.

Our dog lifted his head, sniffed the air, and then lunged forward. His first stop was a nearby pine tree where he lifted his leg and marked the spot. Next, he ate some type of animal scat.

"Duke, gross." I tugged at his leash.

"He's just being a dog," Brad said.

Underneath a clump of trees, Duke pawed pine needles and uncovered a ticket to a recent concert. It wasn't much, but it was a start. I pulled a poop bag out of my pocket. Using the plastic, I picked up the paper and placed the clue inside. "Good job." I slipped our dog a treat. We circled the campsite twice and then rejoined Debbie and Clem.

"Find anything?" Clem asked when we returned.

"We found a ticket to a concert. Pete believes the thieves are kids—might've belonged to one of them. Worth checking out." I wiped the sweat from the back of my neck with my palm.

Debbie set her knitting project down and stood. "I'm so sorry. I should have offered you folks something to drink. Can I get you a bottle of water and a bowl for your dog?"

"No, thanks. We came prepared." I nodded toward the water bottles strapped to our handlebars. "I'll do my best to help you recover your bikes."

We exchanged contact information.

"Thank you. That means a lot," Clem said before we departed.

While we hydrated, I silently berated myself. What had I just agreed to? I'd promised Brad I'd stick it out for a day—but beyond that? My emotions still felt raw from this morning's confession, and I wasn't sure I had the wherewithal to stay on the grounds after the thefts.

"Ready?" Brad asked.

"Let's go." I capped my water and then mounted my bike.

***

The rigorous ride had felt good, and my muscles hummed from the exertion. While Brad showered, I extracted my fingerprint kit from a cabinet and checked the ticket for latent prints. I googled the name of the band and discovered the local group was popular with teens. The venue was a theater in Sumter that seated a maximum of one hundred people. Although the fingerprints were smudged beyond recognition, the clue proved better than my original hopes.

Once I'd washed up, we agreed to take a side excursion to check out the theater before our lunch in Sumter. A quick search on my laptop revealed the perfect place to eat, a pub, Tipsy Tavern, with a dog-friendly patio.

I pulled a lavender cotton T-shirt dress over my head, one of the few non-*cabi* outfits I'd packed for the trip. After I'd laced my white Keds, I spritzed my neck with Amazing Grace and added the dangly earrings I'd purchased at Maria's party.

Brad sniffed the air. "You smell great." He crossed the room and nuzzled my neck. A few more kisses and lunch might have to wait. My stomach grumbled.

Brad laughed. "Hungry?"

"Starving."

"Then let's go." He settled into the driver's seat, started the engine, and drove to our first stop.

Brad and Duke waited in the van while I approached the theater's double glass doors. A crimson awning stretched over the entrance. A blast of cool air greeted me as I stepped inside and scanned the space. Other than a security guard and a woman behind the ticket counter, the building was empty.

"Hello. How can I help you?" the woman asked.

I introduced myself and flashed my PI credentials. "I'm investigating a case. I need a list of attendees from a recent concert."

"You'll have to speak to our director, Sally, about that, and she's not here right now. I can take your contact information and pass it along when she returns. Is there a problem?"

"A ticket from this theater was left behind at the scene of a theft."

Her eyes widened. "Oh, my. That's troubling."

I pulled out a business card and jotted the date of the concert and the name of the band on the back. "I'd appreciate anything Sally can share." I slid my card across the counter.

"I'll make sure she gets this as soon as she comes in."

"Thank you." I nodded and then turned to leave.

As I climbed back into the van, Brad asked, "Any luck?"

"We'll see. The person who could help wasn't in. I left my contact information with the woman at the box office."

Brad pulled away from the curb and took a left onto West Hampton Avenue. He traveled half a mile to the strip center where Tipsy Tavern was located. As we approached, a long, rectangular, taupe brick building with a black-shingled roof came into view. Striped black-and-white awnings sloped over the windows. Underneath, wooden boxes overflowed with black-eyed Susans and purple coneflowers.

In the parking lot behind Tipsy Tavern, we found a spot wide enough for the van. The patio bustled with customers and their pets. After Duke made friends with a golden retriever mix and a tri-colored Australian shepherd, we located a table away from the smokers. Within minutes, a man dressed in a black T-shirt with the bar's logo arrived. He deposited a bowl of ice water next to Duke.

"Hey folks, I'm Robert, the owner, and I'll be your server. Can I start you off with something to drink?" He handed us both a lunch menu along with one for drink selections.

Brad ordered his favorite IPA, and I asked for an iced tea with a splash of sweet tea.

"Got it. Are you ready to order food?"

I perused the laminated card. "What do you recommend?"

"As a starter, the Tipsy Bites are my favorite. We also make a mean burger. If you're in the mood for something healthier, the Greek salad's good."

I glanced at the description of the Tipsy Bites, which included shrimp, jalapeno, and Monterey Jack cheese wrapped in hickory-smoked bacon. "Sounds delicious. Wanna split an order of the bites and the salad?" I asked Brad.

"Sure."

"Trust me. You'll want two orders of the shrimp," Robert interjected.

Brad nodded. "Done."

"And for the pup? We serve Good Boy Dog Beer. It's nonalcoholic, healthy, and we have several flavors."

Brad studied the choices. "How about the chicken-flavored one?" He handed Robert our menus.

"Got it. One Mailman Malt Licker."

As he turned to leave, a young woman burst through the back door. She carried a phone in her hand, and she was no taller than four feet eight inches.

"That bitch," she growled.

"What now?" Robert shrugged. "Sorry folks, meet Racheal, my other half, otherwise known as the Angry Elf."

"Madeleine," she hissed. "Now she claims that she doesn't approve of the new lighted sign—which by the way I already ordered and paid for. *And* she verbally approved. I'm not sure I can return it." She stomped her tiny foot. "Damn her. Next time, I'll get it in writing."

"Who's Madeleine?" I asked, intrigued by the exchange.

Robert interjected. "Our landlady. Racheal and I lease this space from her. If you'll excuse us, I'll place your order with our cook, and she and I will continue this conversation inside."

An afternoon breeze drifted across the patio. Brad and I relaxed in comfortable silence while we waited for our drinks. Outdoor fans were strategically positioned on the weathered wooden deck in case the temperatures became oppressive. Orange umbrellas anchored the center of each wrought-iron table and offered some shade from the sun. I counted about twenty people and half a dozen dogs.

When Robert returned, he set our beverages on the table and then poured the dog beer into a separate bowl for Duke. He leaned forward and said, "So, I went to the aquarium this weekend, but I didn't stay long. There's something fishy about that place."

After I got the dad joke, I doubled over in laughter.

In no time, our food arrived, and I bit into the appetizer. My taste buds tingled in response to the meaty shrimp, melted cheese, and spicy jalapeno wrapped in crunchy bacon and then doused in a sweet and smoky sauce. Duke lapped up every drop of his dog beer.

Once again, I wished that we were staying here in town.

With full stomachs, we strolled around the strip center. Tipsy Tavern anchored the west end. Next door was a barber shop and then an insurance agency. I peered into the window of a neighboring gift shop. Above the wooden door, The Cat's Meow was etched in elegant black script.

Brad noticed my interest. "Go ahead. We'll wait."

When I opened the door, bells jingled, and I stepped inside. Tibetan music resonated within, and the smell of jasmine hung in the air. A graceful silver cat greeted me, and I stroked the feline's back. Tables stacked with tarot cards lined one side of the store, along with racks of T-shirts, embroidered blouses, and easy-to-wear Mexican cotton dresses.

"Hello. Welcome to The Cat's Meow. I'm Sherry, and this is Jazz. How can I help you?" She picked up her cat and cradled it in her arms. Her thick, flowing flaxen hair reached her waistline. She wore an emerald peasant blouse and a multi-layered silver statement necklace. Her whiskey-colored eyes radiated curiosity, and she spoke with a Canadian lilt.

"I'm just browsing. Cute store."

"Thanks. I used to own a restaurant. This is much easier." Sherry put the cat down and brushed the lingering hairs off her sleeve. "Well then, I'll leave you to it. Let me know if you have any questions. Oh, here comes Gypsy." She handed me a wooden basket for my purchases and then scooped up a blue-gray feline. "Gypsy hates to be ignored." The cat purred in response.

Sherry returned to the counter, and I perused a display case filled with antique turquoise jewelry. I meandered to a hutch stocked with baskets of crystals and an assortment of cookbooks. While I read the descriptions of the gems' healing powers, the bells jingled, and a woman who appeared to be about my age strode into the store.

The woman had a commanding presence, like she owned the place. I wondered if she was the landlady Racheal had mentioned. Her sandy-blonde hair was swept into a tight bun, and her icy demeanor screamed bitch. She wore a cream-colored cotton skirt that reached mid-thigh, paired with a lavender silk blouse. I admired her matching lilac patent leather stilettos and well-toned calves.

"Why, hello, Madeleine. To what do I owe this pleasure?" Sherry asked as her cats wove in and out of the woman's legs.

"Would you *please* get your cats away from me?" Madeleine hissed. "And turn off that music." She covered her ears.

Sherry rolled her eyes, lowered the volume with a remote, and then picked up her cats.

"You're officially five days behind on your rent. If you don't have the payment to me by tomorrow, I'll have to assess the five-hundred-dollar late fee."

The tension vibrated in the air, and I made myself busy with the homemade candles that lined the shelves. The one labeled "Golden Gardenia" smelled divine, and I added it to my basket. While I busied myself with a display of wind chimes and dream catchers, I eavesdropped on their conversation.

Madeleine blew on her nails. "Well?"

"Did you just get those done?" Sherry asked. "They look fantastic. I love how they match your blouse."

"Yes, and you didn't answer my question."

"I'll get the money to you. You know, we should *so* get together soon," she crooned. "Have lunch, or do a spa date, *or something*."

Did I detect a hint of sarcasm in the "or something" comment?

Madeleine smiled for the first time. "I'd like that."

While I thumbed through a carousel of greeting cards with photographs of Sumter sights, I caught the scent of Chanel No. 5 as Madeleine exited the store.

"Bitch," Sherry muttered under her breath once Madeleine left. With a flick of the remote, she turned the music back up.

I returned to the jewelry display case and motioned Sherry over. "How much for those?" I pointed at a pair of inlaid turquoise earrings in the shape of a hawk.

"Forty-five dollars."

"I'll take them."

"Are they a gift, or are they for you?"

"For me."

"Oh, those will look fantastic on you." She rang up my purchases. "Sorry about the Madeleine interruption. You know, I'd be happy to do a tarot reading for you. No charge."

"Thank you, but my husband and dog are waiting outside."

She added a couple of peanut-butter-flavored dog biscuits to my bag. "Come back when you have more time."

Outside, I scanned the parking lot for my boys. I fished my phone out of my purse and called Brad. "Where are you?"

"I took Duke for a walk. We're at the restaurant at the opposite end of Tipsy Tavern. Come join us. You need to check out their breakfast menu."

I found the two of them in front of Pecan Creek Grille. My finger followed the long list of breakfast items on the menu posted on the window—tacos, omelets, waffles, pancakes, grits, and bacon. "Looks delicious."

"We should come back in the morning."

I held back the comment I longed to make—*Well, why don't we stay in a nice hotel in Sumter and give up this whole camping thing*—but I bit my tongue.

Brad pointed at the shopping bag. "What'd you buy?"

After I showed him the earrings and candle, I gave our dog one of the biscuits. Duke wagged his tail in gratitude.

Next, we drove around downtown Sumter. An eclectic mix of shops lined both sides of the street, and the signs posted on poles advertised upcoming community events. When we passed a couple entering a historic two-story bed and breakfast with magnificent white columns and a sprawling front porch, I sighed. *That could be us.*

Back at the campground, I filled Duke's bowl with dog food. Brad fixed a Scotch for himself and poured a glass of shiraz for me. As he lit the fire, I queued up the playlist that I'd created for the trip. We listened to "Here Comes the Sun," followed by "Blowin' in the Wind." While the sun descended, casting hues of purple, apricot, and a smoky gray across the horizon, a northern breeze cooled the temperature, and I edged my chair closer to the flames.

When "Moondance" played, Brad stood and offered his hand. Dusk settled in as we swayed to the tune.

When the song ended, Brad took a step back, and his eyes searched mine with an intensity that made my chest tighten. His voice cracked as he whispered, "Thank you for camping with me, after everything you went through." His eyes misted. "Out here... I can almost feel my family's presence."

"You're welcome." I leaned in and gave him a gentle kiss. "I wished that I'd met your parents and your sister," I said, my heart aching for the family I'd never known. I made up my mind to stick it out. Maybe, just maybe, I'd get to know even more about them through Brad's stories on this trip. Duke edged his way between us, breaking the intense moment.

After a second glass of shiraz, I retrieved the macaroni salad from the van's fridge and scooped generous helpings into two plastic bowls. The mixture of macaroni, green onions, eggs, jalapeno, and olives was addictive. I could seriously eat this stuff for breakfast, lunch, and dinner.

The fresh air, full belly, and events of the day caught up with me. I gave Brad a lingering kiss goodnight and was surprised when Duke followed me into the van instead of staying outside with Brad. Maybe he was alternating nights between the two of us.

Around one o'clock in the morning, a nightmare about my Girl Scout trip and the sound of Duke whining jolted me awake. While I took deep calming breaths, I heard the van's door jiggle. My heart stopped, and my breath hitched. Luckily, the vehicle was locked.

I threw back the covers and retrieved my gun from the console. When I peered out the window to check on Brad, I spotted three men in hoodies, retreating from our campsite. I slid the pane open, steadied my shaking hand, and aimed my piece at a nearby tree. The shot resonated. Startled, the three of them ran. I rushed to the vehicle's door, unlocked it, and shoved it open. My heart pounded in my chest, and my palms grew sweaty.

"C'mon, Duke. Let's get the bad guys."

Duke barked and then bolted out the door.

Brad heard the explosion and emerged from the tent. He blinked his eyes. "What was that?"

I pointed ahead. "Those guys were trying to get into our van. I fired a shot to scare them."

The two of us sprinted toward Duke as he raced toward the culprits and latched on to the closest guy's pants. As we closed in, I gasped for air. My husband stood beside me, barely winded, and I pointed my pistol at the perp's head.

"Get your dog off me," the kid screamed. The fabric began to tear as the skinny boy inched his leg forward. Duke growled and tugged at his pant leg.

"Don't you dare move," I said. "Duke, release."

Our dog released his grip and sat by my side while Brad located Pete's number on his cell. He put the phone on speaker.

The park ranger answered after the third ring.

"We caught one of your thieves," Brad said.

"I'll be right there."

In a matter of minutes, Pete arrived and cuffed the perp. Afterward, he nodded his thanks toward Brad and me, patted Duke on the head, and then turned his attention back to the youth. "What's your name, son?"

"Jimmy," he muttered, his voice trembling. His hood had fallen back, revealing a pale face streaked with sweat. The bandana had slipped and exposed cheeks pockmarked with acne scars.

My heart clenched. He looked so young—he couldn't have been more than fifteen. He seemed like a scared kid who'd made a bad choice.

Pete placed his arm around him as he escorted him to the golf cart. "Tell you what, Jimmy. You give me the names of your friends, and I'll put in a good word for you with the police chief."

My chest eased as they departed. At least Duke had eliminated one of the culprits, and it wouldn't be long before the other two were caught. We could relax. Or so I hoped.

Chapter 4

The early morning light filtered through the trees as Brad set off for a run, leaving Duke and me in the quiet of the van. As I hand-washed our coffee mugs in the small sink, my phone pinged with a message from Pete.

Pete: Can you bring Duke down in ten minutes? There's something I'd like to give him.

Me: Sure.

Curious, I abandoned the chore and clipped Duke's leash to his collar. I wondered what surprise awaited him.

When we entered the building, I spotted Pete briefing a group of rangers in crisp uniforms. Duke and I lingered by the door and waited for him to finish. When the employees dispersed to their duties, we approached Pete. He had a wide grin on his face.

"I think your dog earned this." Pete held up a shiny star-shaped badge and then handed the medallion over to me. "I'm happy to report that all three boys are now in juvenile detention." He bent down and patted Duke on the head. "Good boy."

As I accepted the accolade and pinned it onto Duke's harness, a wave of relief washed over me. "Thank you."

"You're welcome." Pete reached into his pocket and peeled the foil off a Hershey's Kiss. "Chocolate is my weakness. Can't get enough of the stuff." He popped the candy into his mouth.

Although I never received that coveted Girl Scout camping badge, Duke had done even better. According to Pete, his unofficial title would be Junior Park Ranger. "What's going to happen to those boys?" I asked.

"I suspect they'll be released to their parents and assigned some type of community service. Returning any stolen goods will also work in their favor."

I hoped that Clem and Debbie would get their bikes back.

When Brad returned from his ride, I shared Duke's new title and what had happened to the kids.

"Good boy." He massaged our dog's ears. "How do you feel about them being locked up in juvie?"

"Mostly relief. But, when I saw how young and terrified that kid was last night, I felt sorry for him. I hope he doesn't get bullied."

"I wanted to punch him for scaring you, but once I'd calmed down, I felt bad for him too."

"At least we don't have to worry about any more robberies." I sighed.

Brad kissed my cheek. "I'm going to take a shower, and then we can try that breakfast place. Care to join me?"

I didn't know if he meant breakfast, the shower, or both, but I immediately followed him into the van's bathroom without asking for clarification.

Pecan Creek Grille also had a dog-friendly patio. The wrought-iron furniture mirrored Tipsy Tavern's. A five-gallon sports cooler filled with water sat atop a rolling cart. The surface was stocked with plastic bowls and a jar of dog biscuits. We took our seats at the only open table.

"Popular place," I commented as I settled into my chair and smoothed the sides of my oversized coral T-shirt.

A tall man in a forest-green apron with the restaurant's logo approached us. "Hi folks, I'm Brock. You can place your orders at the counter." He handed each of us a menu. "There's a large coffee station inside with several flavors. Can't miss it. Cinnamon is our most popular. Help yourself."

"Do you know what you want?" Brad asked after Brock left.

I scanned the choices. "I'll take the All American, eggs scrambled with bacon and grits. No bread."

He stood. "I'll get the coffee and place our order. Do you want the cinnamon?"

I nodded.

While I sipped on a mug of divine spiced coffee laced with milk and sugar, Brad and I chatted about our plans for the day. He wanted to visit a local bike shop that carried a new line of cycling shoes. Since they didn't allow pets, Duke and I'd hang here and wait for his return.

Brock arrived with our food, placed it on the table, and picked up the metal stand with our order number. "Good looking dog." Duke thumped his tail in response. "Where you folks from?"

"Thank you. This is Duke, and I'm Liz—we're visiting from Charleston and camping at Poinsett Park." I patted the surface of the wrought-iron table. "Your patio's identical to Tipsy Tavern."

"Yeah. Our landlady likes the strip center to have a common theme. She says it makes the place look classy." He rolled his eyes. "God forbid I don't deadhead the flowers in the window boxes."

"Is your landlady's name Madeleine?" I asked.

"Yes. Do you know her?"

"No. I've only heard a few of the tenants talk about her."

"Couldn't have been anything good. We're all united in our hatred for that woman." Brock turned to leave. "Enjoy your food."

I bit into the crispy smoke-flavored bacon. Although there was something to be said for breakfast cooked over a campfire, Pecan Creek Grille beat it hands down.

After Brad left for the bike shop, Duke and I meandered down the row of storefronts. I paused at the gift shop, The Cat's Meow, and studied the window display.

Wind chimes and dream catchers hung from strings of crystal beads that reflected a rainbow of colors. Organza in hues of sapphire, teal, and indigo lined the bottom of the shelf. An eclectic mix of cookbooks was stacked on top of the fabric, and a tall black metal tree draped with turquoise necklaces stood next to the arrangement. An assortment of succulents in bronze pots completed the ensemble.

I turned when I heard a car pull into the parking spot behind me. Sherry stepped out of a dark gray Chevy Malibu; each window adorned with white cat paw stickers.

"Liz, you're back." She walked to the passenger's side, pulled out a cat carrier, set it on the sidewalk, and smiled. "Who's this handsome fella?" While my dog sniffed the container, Sherry reached down to pat his head.

"This is Duke."

"Well, hello, Duke. Please come in. Bring your pup. Jazz loves dogs. Gypsy's a little more skittish." She unlocked the door and grabbed the carrier.

"Are you sure?" I did want to check out those Mexican dresses.

"Absolutely. Give me a few minutes to set up shop, and then maybe I can do that reading for you." She flicked on the lights, and a warm glow illuminated the cozy interior.

Duke and I followed her inside. My dog sniffed the unfamiliar smells and wagged his tail in delight.

Sherry unlatched the cat carrier, and Jazz hopped out. Gypsy leapt onto the counter and eyed Duke with a mix of curiosity and caution.

"Make yourself at home. Holler if you need help." Sherry disappeared into the back of the shop.

As I browsed through the clothes rack, Jazz wove in and out of Duke's legs. My fingers skimmed the fabrics and landed on a teal-colored dress embroidered with delicate flowers in fuchsia, coral, red, and lavender.

Sherry reappeared dressed in a royal blue T-shirt emblazoned with the Superwoman logo. She carried a stack of shirts in her arms. "Just got these in—it's my personal motto." She turned to show me the back. Bold white letters declared, "Got a problem? I'll fix it." "Aren't they fantastic?" Sherry laid the merchandise on a nearby table and then noticed my dress selection. "That color would look amazing on you."

The craftsmanship was impeccable. I checked the price tag—two hundred dollars. Not cheap, but probably worth it. I calculated the likely cost per wear in my head.

"Why don't you try it on? I'll watch Duke."

Minutes later, I emerged from behind the curtained dressing room and handed the frock to Sherry. "I'll take it."

"Want me to add one of those T-shirts?"

"Nah. That'll be it."

"Before I ring you up, why don't I do that reading?"

I glanced at my phone. Brad would likely be another thirty minutes. "Sure. Why not?"

She removed Gypsy from the countertop next to the register and spritzed the surface with a spray that smelled like sage.

"What's that?"

"White sage. To clear any negativity."

Duke curled next to my feet. Gypsy slinked against my dog's chest and then settled in next to him.

"Wow. I've never seen my cat do that. Your dog must be special." She lit a white tea candle nestled in rose quartz and closed her eyes. After a moment of silence, she placed a deck of tarot cards on the counter. The jewel-toned images on the cards were framed in gold, and the edges were slightly worn.

"Those are gorgeous. They look antique."

"They're from Ukraine. They were my great-grandmother's cards." Sherry shuffled the deck. "Close your eyes and set an intention." She clarified, "A question you would like an answer to. Please don't say it aloud."

Although I didn't believe in this stuff, I silently complied. *What's in store for us for the rest of this camping trip?*

"Ready?"

I nodded, and she spread the cards face down in a circle. The back was embossed with an elegant black-and-gold paisley design. Before she drew the first card, Sherry moved her hands over the cards in a clockwise and then counterclockwise motion. She stopped, withdrew a card, and placed it face-up in front of me.

"Ah, Justice." The image depicted a woman seated on a throne and clothed in a red cloak with a crown on her head. She held a sword in one hand and a set of scales in the other. "You may be faced with a difficult decision. However, truth and fairness will prevail, and karmic justice will be served."

What the heck did that have to do with camping? And why was I indulging in this silliness to begin with?

Sherry repeated the ritual and then drew a second card. "The Seven of Cups. You'll want to carefully consider the facts. Everything is not as it seems."

Jazz snuggled next to Duke's belly. As the cats purred, she continued. "The information I'm sharing with you may not seem relevant right now. I suggest you journal or spend some time reflecting on the images to gain further insight." She cleared her throat. "One final card." Sherry closed her eyes and tilted her head toward the ceiling. She waited a few seconds before she made her last selection.

When she turned the card over I gasped, and Duke whimpered. The cats scattered. A grim reaper image stared back at me.

"Death." Sherry raised her palm. "Not to worry, dear. This does not signify a physical death." She paused and rubbed her chin. "Although it could, but that's rare. You will likely experience some type of transformation or transition. It's actually a very positive card."

What type of transformation? Was I going to suddenly fall in love with camping? I highly doubted it. "Can I share my earlier question so you can tell me what all of this means?"

"Oh no! That's for you to interpret."

The bells on the front door chimed, and Madeleine stepped inside. Sherry scooped up the deck and blew out the candle. As the nasty woman approached, the cats scurried behind Sherry. Madeleine joined us at the counter and held out her hand. "Check?"

Duke growled.

"Good doggie," Sherry muttered while she fished a checkbook out of her purse.

As Madeleine drummed her fingers on the countertop, she turned toward Duke and tapped her foot on the floor. "Does your dog bite?" She lifted her knee, as if preparing to kick him.

I stepped in between them. "No. Normally, he's very friendly."

Sherry ripped out the rent payment and handed it over.

"Thank you." Madeleine stuffed it in her Gucci handbag. "Now that business is out of the way, we can talk about our get-together."

"Yes. Let's do that. Let me take care of my customer, and then we'll chat."

Sherry rang me up, and Duke and I left. Sherry's demeanor toward Madeleine was puzzling. Her body language conveyed that she couldn't stand the woman, yet her words dripped with sweetness. Was she trying to get in her good graces?

While Duke and I meandered along the sidewalk bordering the businesses, two small dogs pawed at the glass storefront of Joy's Insurance Agency. A woman dressed in a red jacket snapped leashes to their collars and opened the front door. While my dog made friends with the Chihuahua mixes, Madeleine revved the engine of a black Mercedes convertible and sped off, tires screeching.

"What a piece of work." The woman in the red jacket shook her head, then turned back toward the wagging tails.

"Must be in a hurry. Cute dogs."

"This is Maggie and Jemma. Maggie's mine. Jemma belongs to Joy. Oh, and by the way, I'm Ruth." She patted our dog's head. "Who's this friendly guy?"

"This is Duke. You're open on Saturdays?"

"Nope, we're closed. The agency is sponsoring a fun run tomorrow that benefits Carolina Chihuahua Rescue. I'm prepping a few things for the event." She tugged on the dogs' leashes. "C'mon, girls, time to take care of business."

Ruth strode toward a grassy area with a small pond at the front of the strip center. Purple asters and yellow coneflowers adorned the grounds, and a couple of park benches provided a spot to sit and rest.

I checked my phone for messages. Brad had texted that he was on his way and asked me to meet him on the patio of Tipsy Tavern.

I waved at Brad as he approached our table. "Did you find what you were looking for?"

Brad kissed my cheek, then took a seat on the other side of me. "Hey, buddy." He rubbed Duke's ears. "Yeah. They had all the latest gear." He nodded toward my shopping bag. "What'd you buy?"

I pulled out the dress and showed it to him.

"Nice choice. That will look great on you." Brad grinned. "How about we grab a couple of shrimp orders to go, head back to the campsite, and catch some fish?"

It took all my willpower not to visibly wince. I hated fishing, almost as much as I despised camping. "Alright. Duke and I have been here a few minutes, and I've yet to see any waitstaff. Why don't I go inside and place the order? You want anything to drink?"

"Just water. Bring Duke some too."

The sign on the back door read, "No Pets Allowed Inside." Once inside, I blinked a few times to adjust to the dim light.

Racheal was in a heated discussion with a man who towered over her. His auburn hair matched his red nose. Otherwise, the place was empty. She looked my way and held up a finger. "Give me a minute."

"Duncan, you know I can't serve you. You had enough before you got here."

"Jess one more whiskey—for the resh of the game." He slurred his words.

At the front, a big screen played a soccer match. On every wall, TVs flickered with various sporting events. The two-story ceiling gave the space an open, airy vibe. A long bar stretched from the entrance and stopped just shy of the two pool tables in the back.

"Your wife would kill me. You're not allowed to have any drinks here."

Duncan pushed a barstool aside and leaned over the polished ebony counter. "I own diss space too," he hissed, spewing spittle. "My precious Maddie, always in control. But she's not around. C'mon," he pleaded.

"No." Racheal held her ground.

"Fine." He turned and tottered off. "Maybe I'll jess kill her and take care of that witch once and fer all," he muttered.

"Sorry about that. How can I help you?" Racheal said.

I watched the man stagger away. "He's not driving is he?"

"Nah. His wife took his keys away from him months ago. They don't live far from here. What can I do for you?"

I placed the order for our drinks and food, then handed her my card. "Who was that?"

"Our landlady's husband, Duncan. Technically, he's also our land-lord, but he never lifts a finger unless it's to drink a beer or a shot. Guy's got a drinking problem. Although, who can blame him being married to *her*?" She passed the bill over for me to sign. "I'll be right out with your food."

I replayed the conversation in my head. Had Duncan meant it when he said he wanted to murder her? I hoped not. The last thing I needed was to become entangled in a murder investigation.

Chapter 5

Back at the campground at the east end of the lake, we placed our folding chairs by the shoreline, away from the main beach. While Brad threw the tennis ball into the water for Duke to retrieve, I spread a tablecloth on the ground and anchored it with a cooler and a basket laden with napkins, plates, and utensils. I opened the ice chest and poured a generous helping of chardonnay into a tumbler. It was a little early for wine, but this was our last full day in Poinsett, and there was no way I could fish without fortification.

My phone pinged with a group text from my neighbors back home.

Cassie: How's the camping?

Linda: Pictures please!

Maria: With one of your new outfits!

Gwen: Yes! (Smiley face)

I staged two blue plastic plates piled with shrimp, green grapes, Kalamata olives, mac salad, Swiss and cheddar cheese, and club crackers on the red gingham fabric. Before I snapped a photo, I added my stainless steel cup. The response was immediate.

Linda: Whatcha drinking?

Me: Your favorite wine. We're about to go fishing.

Linda: Noooo! You? Fishing?

Duke plopped on the grass, wet and exhausted from his ball-chasing sprints. As he panted, his tongue nearly touched the ground. I grabbed a fishing pole and handed Brad my phone. "Take a picture."

"I took several." He passed the device back.

For our latest adventure, I'd changed into my new *cabi* nautical navy tank paired with denim shorts. I selected the photo with a scowl on my face and hit send. My phone pinged with laugh-out-loud emojis.

Cassie: Maybe for our next game night we can play Go Fish.

Me: Very funny, Sassy Cassie!

Brad and I grabbed our plates and settled into the chairs. The surface of the murky lake reflected the overhead clouds. A Mississippi kite swooped down and caught a dragonfly in midair.

"Is this where you and your dad used to fish?" I asked.

"Yeah. The last time we were here, we snagged several catfish. After Dad and I filleted them, Mom breaded the fillets and then fried them over the campfire." He licked his lips and then frowned. "That was before my sister's accident. We never went fishing again. Dad didn't want to leave Mom at the campground by herself."

"That had to be tough. Is it hard coming back here and reliving those memories?"

"Yes and no. I'm remembering a lot of details that I'd forgotten. I had to stop cycling halfway through my ride today when a wave of grief overcame me. I miss them so much."

My chest grew tight, and my eyes misted. I couldn't imagine. I reached over and squeezed his hand. Several moments of silence passed before I asked, "Um... Are we going to keep what we catch? I mean, we have plenty of food." I drew a hard line when it came to cutting up slimy fish.

"Nah. Probably release what we hook."

After I exhaled the breath I'd been holding, I took a gulp of wine. "Where's the bait?"

"No bait. We'll use barbless hooks... Less damage to the fish."

The handful of times I'd gone fishing, I'd never caught anything, and I doubted this time would be any different, but I asked, "Will you help me release anything I catch?"

Brad nudged my elbow with his hand. "Sure." He grinned. "Wuss."

I playfully slapped his hand. "Hey, I'm here aren't I?"

Three hours and five catfish later, we called it an afternoon. Surprisingly, I'd caught two of them.

"Thank you for fishing with me. It meant a lot."

I looked down at my feet, ashamed of my earlier bad attitude. "You're welcome." I leaned over and kissed him.

After our non-fish dinner, a feast of chicken and veggie kebabs roasted over the campfire, I snuggled next to Brad in the sleeping bag. The rustle of leaves whispering in the breeze created a soothing contrast to the chaos of the past few days. The thieves were gone, and as I drifted off to sleep, I reflected on our trip and Sherry's reading. Maybe karmic justice was served when Duke caught the thief. I wasn't sure about the meaning of the other cards, but I'd survived our camping trip, and I felt a sense of peace about the past. Tomorrow would be our last day in the park. Spending time with Brad and our dog out in the woods had been OK, and I cherished the memories that he'd shared.

The next morning, Brad left for one last swim in the lake. After I'd packed most of our gear, I snapped Duke's leash to his collar, and we followed the dirt road down to the station to say goodbye to Pete.

He greeted us as soon as we stepped inside. "Well, there's my favorite junior ranger." Pete scratched Duke's head and then reached inside his shirt pocket to offer him a treat.

"We came to say our goodbyes and thank you for all that you do."

"I hope you folks will come back soon."

"My husband loves this park. I'm sure we'll be back." As I extended my hand, a camper burst through the door, his face pale.

"There's a dead body down at the lake!" he shouted.

As Pete reached for his phone, my chest tightened.

The man added, "Someone already called 911."

My stomach dropped. "Who is it?" I managed to ask.

"Some woman."

I breathed a huge sigh of relief that it wasn't Brad. Pete rushed toward his golf cart, and Duke and I dashed after him. "Can we come with you? Brad's down there."

"Hop in." We jumped into the passenger side of the golf cart, and Pete sped toward the scene as fast as the vehicle would go—which was only about thirty miles an hour. I held Duke close as we bumped down the road.

Red lights flashed in front of us as an ambulance rushed toward the shore. When we arrived, Pete scurried off to speak with the cops. I scanned the small crowd of people. Where was Brad? I finally spotted him near the spot where we'd fished yesterday. He stared down at the limp body of a woman dressed in a green-and-pink top and white capris streaked with algae.

Duke and I rushed to his side. "What happened?"

"I was stretching in the water after swimming laps," he gasped.

Duke looked at Brad and whined.

"I'll be alright, boy." He patted Duke's head.

Brad's ashen face didn't look OK to me.

He found his voice and continued. "I couldn't have been more than waist-high when I stepped on something that felt like a body. I reached down and discovered a leg. After I pulled the woman ashore, I tried to revive her, but she was already gone." Brad whispered, "If my sister had lived to be her age, she would've looked just like her." He doubled over and threw up the contents of his stomach.

Kristin, his sister, who'd died in a drowning accident in their family pool. As I rubbed my husband's back, I took a closer look at the corpse. My hand flew to my mouth when I realized it was the same woman who'd sped off in the black convertible yesterday—Madeleine. I turned my focus back to my husband, who had just been re-traumatized.

A police SUV with *Sumter Dive Team* emblazoned on the side parked beside the ambulance. The divers suited up and then waded into the murky water toward the spot where Brad had discovered the body. On the beach, a team of investigators began to capture images of potential evidence, take measurements, and bag items of interest.

A female officer in a black uniform approached us. "Sir, I understand you're the person who discovered the body. I'm sure this has been quite a shock, but I'll need to take your statement."

She continued, "I imagine that you'd like to leave after witnessing that."

Pete must've mentioned that it was our last day in the park.

"But, if you could stay a few more days, in case we need additional information, it'd be greatly appreciated."

A few more days? I brushed the dirt with the sole of my shoe in frustration.

Brad said, "Of course we'll stay. I'll help however I can. Who was she?" Duke stayed glued to Brad's side as if he had a sixth sense about the situation.

"I'm sorry, sir. We haven't identified the body yet."

While the authorities secured the area between the road and the lake with yellow tape, the officer took Brad's statement, and the coroner's vehicle arrived.

Pete strode toward us and waved at the officer. "Howdy, Jane."

"Hey there, Pete. Been awhile."

When Pete caught a glimpse of the corpse, he took a step back. "Damn. That's Madeleine." He tugged on the end of his mustache before adding, "There will be a lot of folks happy to know that *she's* dead."

***

When we returned to the campsite, I lit a fire. Duke instinctively planted himself next to a shivering Brad. I draped a blanket over his shoulders and handed him a bottle of cold water. After he'd recovered from the initial shock, I said, "That had to be awful for you. What do think about going home?"

"Not until we find out what happened to that woman." He set his jaw.

"It was probably an accident. Maybe she slipped and fell?"

"I don't think so. More likely foul play. Either way, we need to find out the truth."

"You're right." My aversion to camping was clouding my better PI judgment. The image of the Death tarot card popped into my head, along with Sherry's comments about the card rarely symbolizing an actual loss of life. "I'll walk to the station and let them know we'll be staying."

"Take Duke."

"Alright, but let's get you into a hot shower first."

Once I was comfortable that Brad was settled, Duke and I left for the station. When we arrived, Pete was in a deep conversation with a member of the Sumter police. As I attempted to eavesdrop, Pete glanced my way and held up a finger, signaling for me to give him a minute.

After the officer left, Pete refilled his coffee and poured a cup for me. "How's your husband?" Before waiting for a reply he added, "Cream, sugar?"

"Both, please. He'll be OK. I guess we're going to be sticking around a few more days."

"I figured as much." He handed me the mug. "We're not full. You can keep the same spot."

I blew on the hot liquid and seized the challenge of discovering what happened to the woman. "I saw how Madeleine treated people. She seemed harsh, but you said there'd be a lot of people happy that she was dead. Why?"

"She's made more enemies than friends. Madeleine's my nephew's wife—and the reason he's the town drunk. She belittled him every chance she got."

Pete unwrapped a Hershey's Kiss, popped it into his mouth, and crumpled the foil wrapper in his hand. "Maddie's mom died when she was a wee one. Her dad, George, was one of my best friends. He passed away from a heart attack about ten years ago."

"I'm so sorry."

"Thanks." Pete's facial features softened. "Everyone loved George. The kindest man you'd ever meet. He owned a bunch of properties around town. If a tenant couldn't pay the rent, he'd find a way to help them out. When he died, Madeleine took over." He shook his head. "Don't know how she turned out the way she did. There wasn't an ounce of compassion in her soul."

As I sipped the strong brew, I waited for Pete to elaborate.

"It doesn't help that my nephew is always drunk, and all the responsibility fell on Madeleine's shoulders."

"Do you think someone murdered her?" I lowered my mug. The circumstances of her death seemed out of the ordinary.

"I wouldn't be surprised. My niece-in-law wasn't a nice person. She carried a lot of resentment and made everyone around her pay for it. Lord knows why." Pete scratched his head. "It's possible she accidentally slipped and drowned, but..." He hesitated, then continued. "Why was she even out at the lake? I can't see her voluntarily coming to the park. They had a South Carolina All Park Passport, but that was more Duncan's thing. He liked to fish."

"Um, Brad and I were at the Tipsy Tavern. I overheard Duncan saying he wanted to murder her. If she *was* killed, do you think Duncan did it?"

Pete shrugged and looked at his leather boots. "I hate to say it, but maybe. My nephew's a carpenter and a talented pianist. And of course, Maddie hates music. She sold his piano a year after they were married." He corrected himself. "Hated. The two of them were opposite in every way imaginable. I never understood it." Pete checked his watch and sighed. "Chief Clayton's on his way. I promised I'd go with him to deliver the news to Duncan."

I took that as my cue to leave.

When I returned to the van, a half-naked Brad emerged from the bathroom, towel-drying his hair. Even though my heart ached for what he'd just endured, I couldn't help but admire his sculpted chest and toned abs.

I pulled back the drapes that concealed the small whiteboard and corkboard on the opposing wall. From a cupboard, I extracted markers and index cards. The death could've been accidental, but my gut said no.

I was determined to solve this as quickly as possible and return to the comfort of our home.

Brad fixed a cup of coffee and settled on the padded bench behind me. I heard Duke hop up next to him. "I see you're on it. Did the park hire you?"

"Nope. This one's pro bono." After the sale of Brad's identity theft protection company, we were set for life. Whenever I took a paid job, I donated the proceeds to charity.

At the top of the whiteboard, I wrote "Suspects." As I penned Duncan's name, I recalled his murderous words at the Tipsy Tavern. And then I remembered Brock's statement that all the tenants were united in their hatred for the woman. I added Sherry, Brock, Ruth, Racheal, and Robert to the suspect list.

Next to "Suspects," I made a list of questions. *How did the body get in the lake? How do park passes work? Where are the entrances to the property?*

"Will you hand me that packet that Pete gave us when we arrived? It should be in one of the seat pockets."

Brad handed me the folder filled with information about the park, and I pulled out the map. The document illustrated two entrances, the main one and another for the rangers' residences in the back. I pinned the map onto the corkboard.

Inside the packet, I found a form to order a park passport along with a sheet of "Frequently Asked Questions." Not all the South Carolina state parks required registration when you entered the property, especially if you only stayed the day. Poinsett Park was one of them. I added a column titled "To Do's" and penned *Get the name of the medical examiner.* I prayed that a rush had been put on the results. Pete seemed to have a good relationship with the local cops, and I needed an insider. I jotted *Buy chocolate for Pete.* Even though he owed us one for solving the thefts, it wouldn't hurt to sweeten him up with some candy. We'd met Brock, Ruth, Sherry, Racheal, and Robert, but we hadn't met the owner of the strip center's barber shop, so I wrote *Brad— haircut* underneath.

He studied the board. "Why am I getting a haircut? What does that have to do with the woman's death?"

"Pete's convinced the body is his niece-in-law, Madeleine." I continued, "She was also the landlady for the strip center where Tipsy Tavern is located. Eventually, I'll need to interview all the tenants."

"When do we start?"

"Are you sure you're up for this?" I studied his face.

His eyes narrowed, and he clenched his jaw. "One hundred percent."

I playfully poked him in the chest. "Get dressed. We'll visit the barbershop first."

"With Duke?"

"Of course." Our dog's truth-detecting skills would come in handy.

I glanced at my watch—ten o'clock. "Let's visit Madeleine's home. I'd like to see where they live in relation to the center." Even without Duncan's damning words, the husband was always a good place to start. "Then you can get that haircut."

Chapter 6

While Brad drove, I googled Madeleine's last name, Collins, and then located the address. We parked the Sprinter down the street, a few houses away from the couple's home. On the van's floor, Duke gnawed on a rawhide.

"Let's see if we can catch any of the conversation." I adjusted the volume on the state-of-the-art audio amplifier and silently thanked my husband for anticipating everything someone in my profession might need. Next, I extracted a camera and a pair of binoculars from the console and handed the spyglasses to Brad. A police car blocked Duncan's driveway, and a tall Black male cop with closely cropped white hair stood next to Pete at the front door.

While Chief Clayton delivered the news of Madeleine's death, I zoomed in to study Duncan's face. His red-rimmed eyes grew wide, yet he didn't seem shocked that his wife was dead.

My pulse quickened as Clayton's words piped into the van's speakers.

"Son, when's the last time you saw your wife?"

"Yesterday. She said she was going to dinner at a friend's house." Duncan ran his hand through his auburn hair. "Damn. She's always awake before me. I didn't think anything of it when I didn't see her this morning. Are you sure she's dead?"

"Sorry, Dunc. Saw her myself," Pete said.

"In the lake at Poinsett? She hated that place." He rubbed his forehead.

The police chief motioned toward the car. "C'mon, son, put your shoes on. Since you're next of kin, we need you to identify the body."

While Duncan turned to fetch his footwear, Brad started the engine and pulled away before anyone could spot us.

He reached over and squeezed my hand. "Duncan didn't strike me as a grieving husband. If anything ever happened to you, I'd be devastated."

"Me too. It's early, but I agree. While you were in the shower, Pete filled me in on their relationship. It wasn't good. Duncan's the town drunk, and it sounded like she made his life miserable."

***

The words "Southern Scissors" were painted in red script over a pair of large black scissors on the barbershop's picture-glass window. The sign at the entrance stated that walk-ins were welcome.

Brad pulled the door open. A woman who appeared to be in her sixties greeted us. She wore a taupe apron adorned with the shop's scissor logo. Above the symbol, the name "Michelle" was embroidered in black thread. Three styling stations lined either side of the small space, and the smell of hair tonic hung in the air. A pop tune streamed through speakers mounted on the walls.

Michelle motioned us inside. "Come in. What can I do for y'all?"

"Is it OK if we bring our dog?" I asked.

"Of course. Look at that cutie. What's his name?"

"Duke," Brad replied. "I'd like to get a haircut."

"Hello, Duke." As Michelle scratched his back, our dog wagged his tail, scattering hair from an earlier appointment across the floor. "DZ, cut," she hollered toward the back. A man in a matching apron emerged from the back with a coffee mug in his hand.

"This is my husband, DZ."

He shook Brad's hand and then mine. DZ offered a palm to Duke, who promptly placed his paw in it. Once the introductions were complete, he asked, "Who's getting the cut?"

I pointed at Brad. DZ led him to a chair, draped a smock over Brad's chest, and snapped it around his neck. While DZ adjusted the height of the stool, I found a seat on the other side of the station. Duke sprawled out underneath my legs on the cool tile floor.

"So, what's DZ stand for?" I asked.

As if on cue, Kenny Loggins' "Danger Zone" blared through the speakers. DZ grinned, grabbed his shirt collar, and shook his hips. "That's me." He winked and launched into the chorus.

When the moment passed, he clarified, "Actually it's David Zachariah." He picked up a comb and ran it through Brad's hair. "Same style?"

Brad nodded.

"How much you want cut off?"

"Half an inch," Brad replied.

I glanced around the empty shop. "Slow day?"

Michelle approached Brad's chair. "We have a full afternoon of appointments, but so far this morning has been quiet. Hopefully, we'll get more walk-ins. Can I get you anything to drink? Coffee? Water?"

Brad shook his head.

"No, thank you," I replied and then sighed. "Our day's been crazy."

DZ picked up his shears while I continued, "My husband discovered a dead body in the lake in Poinsett Park."

Michelle gasped and placed her hand over her heart. She leaned in, her eyes wide. "Oh, my Lord. A dead body?"

Duke whined.

Unfazed, DZ began snipping.

"Yes. It was supposed to be the last day of our camping trip. Brad was taking one last swim in the lake when he found her."

"How awful. You poor dear." Michelle patted Brad's hand. "Any idea who it was?"

"The park ranger said it's some woman named Madeleine."

Michelle recoiled, and DZ dropped his scissors. The shears clattered to the floor and startled Duke. He barked and then darted behind my chair.

"Did she have long, sandy-blonde hair? In her late thirties?" Michelle asked while DZ retrieved the shears.

"Yeah," Brad replied. "Do you know her?"

"Maybe. Sounds a lot like our landlady. I just did a lash touch-up for her yesterday. She was excited about going to a friend's house for a sushi dinner."

"You do lash extensions?" I asked. It seemed like an odd service for a barber shop.

Michelle caught my puzzled expression. "We started offering them two years ago. It's made a huge difference to our bottom line. I'm the only esthetician in Sumter who's trained."

"What time was Madeleine here?" I asked.

"Her appointment was at two. Of course, she arrived twenty minutes late—typical Madeleine." She rolled her eyes.

So far, Duke hadn't yipped once.

DZ resumed snipping. As locks of Brad's hair fell to the floor, I asked, "How long have you been tenants here?"

"Since the beginning," DZ said as he cut. "The original owner, Madeleine's dad, George, was great. Gave us a big break when our son passed." He paused, setting the scissors on the metal tray and reached over to squeeze Michelle's hand. "Brain cancer. For months we struggled just to get through each day. George gave us the time we needed, and he always sent a card on the anniversary of our son's death."

"And then Madeleine took over," Michelle spewed. "Before we added the lash services, we struggled to pay the rent. That woman had no mercy. Honestly, if that's who died, I'm not sad that she's gone." No yip from Duke.

"Did she drown?" DZ asked.

"Probably. There were no visible wounds, but we don't know for sure." I pressed on. "Did Madeleine mention where she was going after her appointment?"

Michelle shook her head. "Why are you asking?"

"Sorry. Curious by nature."

Michelle considered my comment for a moment and then said, "Well, I got the impression that she didn't want to say who she was meeting for dinner. Maybe a boyfriend? Her relationship with her husband wasn't the best."

DZ finished Brad's cut, then brushed stray hairs off his neck. He handed Brad a mirror. "What do you think?"

"Not bad. Thanks."

Before Michelle returned to the front desk to take care of a customer, I asked, "Do you have other employees?"

"Yes. Two others—Jae and Jessica. They've been with us for years."

After Brad paid the bill and added a generous tip, we stepped outside.

"Looking handsome." I leaned into Brad, and he pulled me close. As our lips pressed together, my nerves tingled, and warmth spread throughout my body. Brad's stomach grumbled, and I reluctantly pulled away. "Hungry?"

"Starving, and I could use a cold beer. Let's grab lunch at the Tavern."

"Great idea."

I was amazed at how well Brad was holding up after this morning's shock. The owner, Racheal, struck me as the nosy type, and I had a hunch that she kept a close watch on all the comings and goings of the center. Maybe she'd have some dirt on the tenants' relationship with Madeleine.

We walked hand in hand to the back patio and ordered lunch. After Brad devoured a hamburger and onion rings, and I finished my Cobb salad, I stood. "I'm going inside to chat with Robert and Racheal. You and Duke good?"

He nodded, and I left while he sipped on his second beer.

Inside, an older man sat at the far end of the bar with a newspaper spread out in front of him. He appeared to be working a crossword puzzle. Not a single patron occupied the tables scattered throughout the space.

Behind the bar, Racheal thumbed through an Asian cookbook, while Robert wiped down the sleek ebony counter with a rag.

I slid my empty iced tea glass across the bar top. "Can I get a refill?"

"Of course. Unsweet with a splash of sweet tea?" Robert asked.

"Yes, please." I loved servers who remembered your favorites.

He leaned in as he handed me my drink. "How long are you staying at the park?"

"We were supposed to leave today, but my husband discovered a dead body in the lake this morning."

Racheal turned around, and her eyes grew wide. She picked up a backpack and stuffed the Asian cookbook inside.

"A body?" Robert waved at the man at the end of the bar. "David, join us."

Racheal cozied up next to Robert, and David took the seat on the other side of me.

"This is my dad, David," Racheal said.

"Nice to meet you. Are you the cook? The food's fantastic."

He nodded. "That would be me and thank you. So, what's going on?"

Robert chimed in, "Liz said her husband found a dead body in the lake at the park."

David flinched and then stammered. "A dead person?... In Poinsett Park?"

"Yeah, it's troubling, to say the least," I said.

"Was it a camper?" Robert asked.

"Nope," I replied. "The park ranger said it's your landlady, Madeleine."

Robert grinned and did a little happy dance. "Ding-dong, the bitch is dead."

Racheal chewed on her lower lip. "Was she murdered?"

The contrast of their reactions was puzzling. "They don't know. Could've been an accident."

"I bet she was murdered." Robert extracted a composition notebook from a drawer and slapped it on top of the bar. "Plenty of people with motive."

"Robert, give me that!" Rachael lunged for the black-and-white bound book, but Robert slid it out of reach.

"My daughter has an unhealthy obsession." David clucked his tongue.

"What do you mean?" I asked, perplexed.

Racheal responded, "My dad doesn't like that I record all of Madeleine's wrongdoings. I thought it'd come in handy if we ever decided to sue the witch." She shrugged. "Guess that won't be happening."

Robert opened the journal to a random page and tapped his finger on the handwritten words. I noticed a doodle of a knife dripping with blood in the margin. "Here's a good example. The owners of Pecan Creek Grille, Brock and Stacey, hired a high school student who has a speech impediment to work the front counter. Racheal was there when Madeleine ordered something from him. She kept telling him to spit his words out."

"Wow, that's horrible, but it's hardly cause for murder," I said.

"Oh, it gets better." Robert leaned forward and placed his elbows on the counter. "A couple of years ago, Brock and Stacey were renovating the restaurant. When some of the materials got delayed, Madeleine threw a hissy fit. She insisted that everything had to be done in time for the center's Fall Festival." Robert air quoted the words "Fall Festival." "Our wicked witch landlady demanded that he stay and supervise the completion of the work—so, he delayed a trip to Georgia to visit his mom. A week later, his mom died of a heart attack. She never apologized or sent her condolences."

"That's terrible." I took a long sip of my tea and wished the bar allowed pets inside. Was everything in the notebook accurate or did Racheal like to embellish?

"OK. That's enough." She attempted to wrench the journal from Robert's hands. "I'm sure Liz doesn't want to hear all of this."

"Please keep going," I said.

Robert opened another random page. "Oh, this one's *really* bad. A year ago, Madeleine ran over one of Sherry's cats. Killed it. Racheal witnessed the whole thing. The woman drove off without even checking to see if it was dead or alive."

If all this was true, Madeleine was truly evil.

Racheal continued, "I was trying to find something to put Karma's body in when Duncan arrived. Madeleine must have called him. He stuffed her into a large shoebox, covered the body with paper towels, and took the box to Sherry's shop." She shook her head. "Karma was a beautiful long-haired black cat. She was only two. It was so sad."

My hand flew to my chest. I couldn't imagine being so heartless and then leaving your husband to clean up the mess. "What about Madeleine's relationship with the other tenants?"

"Racheal records every single infraction that woman makes." Robert corrected himself. "Made." He returned to the notebook and thumbed through more pages. I caught a glimpse of a sketch of a skull and crossbones.

I pointed at the ink drawing. "Is that a skull and crossbones?"

"I'll admit that I've had a few of my own murderous thoughts about her," Racheal said. "But if she was killed, it wasn't me."

Once again, I wished that Duke was by my side.

Before Racheal could say more, a group of twenty-somethings entered the bar and took a seat at a table in the front.

David shuffled off to the kitchen, and Robert excused himself and strode toward the table with a stack of menus.

I set my empty tea glass on the counter. "If she was murdered, you'll want to turn that notebook over to the cops."

She shrugged. "Yeah, maybe. You ready to close out your check?"

"Yes, please."

As she handed me the bill, she said, "Come back, and your next order of Tipsy Bites is on me."

When I returned to the patio, Brad's forehead rested on his arms as he softly snored. I gently nudged him. "Let's go back to the campsite. You've had enough excitement for today."

Chapter 7

In the van's bed, Brad softly snored with Duke curled at his feet. After I jotted a note on a Post-it and stuck it on the door, I cycled back to the lake. I parked my bike next to the yellow tape that cordoned off the area where Brad had discovered the body. The midday sun glared as I paced the perimeter.

The scene was dotted with footprints from the earlier crowd. While I scanned the murky water, I imagined the possibilities. Was she alive or dead when she got here? Possibly drugged? Maybe someone drove into the park late at night and dumped the body. How did she get into the lake? Did she decide to take a swim, or did someone carry her into the water?

My eyes landed on the boathouse on the opposite shore. I made a mental note to check it out and question the campers closest to the site. Maybe someone heard something.

I rubbed my chin. Who was strong enough to lift a five-foot-six-inch woman? Madeleine was fit, but I guessed that she weighed at least one hundred and twenty-five pounds. And if she was dead, she would've felt heavier. Possibly Duncan, Brock, Robert, or even DZ. Racheal likely lugged heavy kegs around the bar, but with their differences in height, carrying the body would have been a challenge.

As I scrutinized the area, I noticed a set of tire tracks close to the beach's edge. I edged closer and studied the indentation. A glint of silver by the water caught my attention. Was that leftover foil from a Hershey's Kiss? Although Pete had likely munched on one this morning, I mentally added him to the list of suspects. He was strong enough, and he had full access to the park.

The tire tracks pointed toward Park Road, so I hopped back on my bike and pedaled in that direction. Once I rounded the bend, the staff residences came into view. Which one was Pete's? My legs pumped as I navigated farther down the bumpy road to the residents' main entrance. A lone sign marked the location, and cattle gates blocked access to the highway. Upon closer inspection, I noted the absence of a lock. Anyone could've entered the park undetected.

As I cycled back toward camp, I searched for cameras. There were a few in the residences' area, but they weren't pointed at the road. My gut told me her death wasn't accidental. How could I narrow the growing list of suspects and solve the case in record time? I longed to be back in Charleston in the comfort of our home.

Duke and I needed to chat with Pete. I had to know if he could be trusted. The bag of chocolates I'd purchased when we'd restocked our groceries for the extended trip would provide an excuse for the unexpected visit.

Careful not to wake Brad, I slipped back into the van. I quickly penned another note and placed it on top of the first one, then snatched the sweets and coaxed Duke outside. He wagged his tail as he trotted along the road leading toward the station.

When we entered the building, Pete was behind the counter speaking with a skinny teenager who looked a lot like the thief we'd apprehended.

The boy spotted my dog and backed up toward the wall. "He's not going to try and bite me is he?"

"As long as you're not doing something suspicious, Duke's very friendly." I shot Pete a puzzled look.

"Our thieves have been assigned to do community service in the park. Jimmy has taken an interest. Thinks he might want to be a ranger one day." Pete put his arm around the boy's shoulder.

Jimmy hung his head, and his cheeks flushed. "Ma'am, I'm real sorry about scaring you."

I thought for a moment and then said, "Apology accepted. Just promise me you'll stay out of trouble."

Jimmy shuffled his feet. "Yes, ma'am."

I hoped this was a turning point for the teenager. "Would you like to pet Duke?"

"OK." Jimmy stepped from behind the worktop. Pete followed.

Duke and I inched toward them. When we were a few feet away, I said, "Duke, sit."

Jimmy looked at Pete, then me and slowly approached my dog with his right palm extended. Duke's tail thumped on the floor, and he licked the boy's hand.

"Good dog." The teenager scratched Duke's ears and patted his head.

"Son, it's 'bout time you get back out there with your buddies and pick up the trash. Go on, now." He shooed him away.

"Yes, sir. Bye, Duke." Jimmy gave him one last pat on the head.

Once the teen departed, Pete said, "What brings you here?"

"I brought you some treats." At the word "treat," Duke's tail wagged double-time. "Not for you, buddy." I addressed Pete, "Thought you could use them after this morning."

"Much appreciated." He inspected the bag of Hershey's Kisses. "Dark chocolate. I haven't tried that one. Bet it tastes good with a cup of coffee. Can I make you a cup?" He set the bag on the countertop.

I was past my caffeine limit for the day, but his offer gave me an excuse to stick around and ask questions. "Sounds great."

Pete returned with two mugs filled with steaming liquid.

I placed mine on top of the workspace. "That's a positive development with the teens. Do you think they'll behave?"

"I hope so. The boys turned over the stolen goods to the cops, and they sure seemed remorseful." He rubbed his chin. "I have a good feeling about it, especially Jimmy. Going to take that boy under my wing. Who knows, maybe someday he'll be a ranger." Pete blew on his coffee and took a sip. "How's Brad?"

"He's taking a nap. This morning took a toll on him. His sister accidentally drowned when she was just a kid."

"Damn. That must've been traumatic."

"Your Madeleine looks a bit like her. That shook him up." My chest grew tight as I considered the trauma my husband had experienced. I gave in to temptation, lifted the cup, and sipped the brew. "Have you heard anything about the cause of her death?"

"Yep. The chief's keeping me in the loop. We've been friends since grade school. Preliminary report from the coroner places her dead before she entered the water. But you didn't hear me say that."

"Any idea what time she died?"

"Time of death is estimated to be around nine p.m., give or take."

"What about cause?"

Pete tugged on one end of his walrus mustache. "You sure do ask a lot of questions."

After I divulged my profession, he nodded his approval. "Suppose we could use an extra hand to get to the bottom of this. OK if I let the chief know?"

I fished a business card out of my back pocket and handed it to him. "Of course."

Pete continued. "No visible wounds or trauma to the head. It will take a while to get the toxicology reports back. The preliminary analysis of the tire tracks by the lake wasn't much use. Fairly common, likely a midsize sedan."

"Anything else?"

"The divers did find her purse at the bottom of the lake, but any history on her cell phone is toast. Clayton is working on getting the records from her provider."

As if on cue, Pete's phone rang. "You're going public that this is a murder investigation? Damn. That will probably vacate the park." He glanced my way. "Listen, turns out the wife of the man who found the body is a private investigator. She wants to help." Pete handed the phone to me.

After I explained my credentials and gave the chief a summary of my experience, he asked about my rates. "No charge. I'm happy to do this for free."

"You'll need to sign a contract. I need to pay you something," the chief replied.

We finally settled on a token fee of one dollar. I shared my contact details and returned the phone to Pete.

"Guess you're hired," he said after he ended the call. "Any more questions for me? Chief's making a public statement about this being a murder investigation in an hour. I need to get ready for the mass exodus."

"Has anyone checked the park's security footage?"

"I did. Nothing to note, unless you count a family of raccoons raiding the trash." Pete tore open the bag of Kisses, unwrapped a chocolate, and tossed it into his mouth. "Damn. That's good." He chased the candy down with a gulp of coffee and offered one to me.

"No thanks." I waved off the sweet. "Earlier, I cycled the trail that leads to the onsite residences. Who lives there?"

"Me and a few other park rangers and their spouses. Why do you ask?"

"I noticed a back entrance, behind the residences. Just wondering if anyone heard or saw someone driving that way last night."

He shook his head. "The cops already questioned everyone. Nobody saw nothing, including me. I slept straight through the night."

So far, Duke hadn't yipped once, and I silently thanked God that I could eliminate Pete from the long list of suspects.

"What about the boathouse? Is it possible that someone used one of the boats to dump her body?"

"Unlikely. If someone took one of our boats, they'd need to bring their own paddles." He pointed toward a storage closet. "We keep ours locked up in there. Campers pay a fee and sign a waiver before we hand over the oars."

As our dog led the way back to our campsite, I sighed. One suspect down—and at least nine more to go.

Brad was in front of the van, stretching his hamstrings. Outfitted in nylon shorts and a royal blue Ironman T-shirt, he was dressed for a run. Duke rushed to his side. "Not this time, buddy. I need to burn off some steam." He ruffled our dog's fur. "How was your visit with Pete?"

I caressed his shoulder. "Pete told me that the coroner said she was dead before she entered the water. There was no way you could've saved her."

Brad took a deep breath. "Thank you for that." He kissed my cheek and then took off in the direction of the trail.

Duke and I headed the opposite way, toward the boathouse. Despite Pete's doubts, I wanted to check it out for myself. The weathered wooden structure, tucked against the shoreline, housed half a dozen canoes and a few kayaks anchored in place with rusted chains. A wooden roof protected the boats from scorching sun and pouring rain. A faint scent of algae and damp wood lingered in the air, as Duke's nose worked overtime on the deck.

I leaned over each vessel and looked for something the cops might have missed, finding only damp leaves and traces of mud. Anything else had either been nonexistent or bagged as evidence.

Duke's sharp bark interrupted the silence. My heart raced until I discovered the culprit—a bullfrog, as it leapt from one lily pad to the next. I laughed when Duke barked for the second time. "C'mon, boy." I gave his leash a gentle tug. "Let's see if any of the campers saw or heard anything."

A handful of campsites dotted the shoreline. I approached the nearest tent and introduced myself to an older couple. As we chatted by their firepit, I explained that my husband was the one who found the body, and that I was a PI assisting with the investigation.

"Why is there an investigation?" the woman asked. "I thought she drowned."

"Just a precaution."

Duke yipped.

Both claimed they didn't hear or see anything out of the ordinary.

Two sites over, a younger couple played cards at a picnic table. When I asked if they'd seen anyone down at the boathouse last night, they shook their heads.

None of the other campsites were occupied. Maybe the news of her murder had already leaked out. Although my gut said the perp didn't take the risk of hauling one of the park's boats onto the lake, I made a mental note to ask Chief Clayton for the evidence log.

Back in the van, the late afternoon sun streamed through the windows. I kicked the air conditioning down a notch and faced the whiteboard. Duke curled up on the floor for a snooze.

Uncapping the black marker, I added a column titled "Knowns" and listed what we'd learned from the day. *Madeleine had dinner with a friend. Time of death around 9:00 p.m. Dead before entering the water. No blunt trauma or gunshot wounds.* Next, I noted my findings from the lake.

Under "Questions," I penned *How did she die? Who was the friend she was meeting for dinner? Did she drive or catch a ride? Where was her car now?* I studied the list and then wrote; *Who drives a midsize sedan?* I recalled Sherry's Malibu and jotted the information on the board.

Hmmm, what about Duncan? I texted Pete.

Me: What type of car does your nephew drive?"

Pete: A Jeep. As far as I know, he hasn't driven it in months. Maddie took the keys away.

Back to "Knowns" I added *Tire tracks led toward the back entrance. Racheal keeps a log of all of Madeleine's wrongdoings. Duncan drives a Jeep.*

To the "Suspects" list, I added *Stacey* from Pecan Creek Grille, *Ruth* from the insurance agency, *DZ, and Michelle* from the barbershop, and I erased *Buy chocolate for Pete* and *Brad haircut* from my list of "To-Do's."

I numbered the potential suspects. Duncan earned the number one spot, followed by Racheal and Robert from Tipsy Tavern and then Brock and Stacey. After I'd questioned everyone on the list, I'd have a clearer sense of my next move.

Next, I placed a call to my ex-boss and mentor, Gunner, to get his take on the case. I respected his sharp observation skills and attention to detail, and he had a knack for giving me the guidance I needed, exactly when I needed it.

"Yo, Liz. What's up?"

"I need your take on a murder investigation."

"Shoot."

As I explained the situation, Gunner interrupted me. "Wait, what? You're camping?"

Yeah, it was obvious that wasn't my style. "It's a long story. But the sooner I can get out of here, the better."

"I know Sumter's police chief, Clayton. He's a good guy, capable, well respected by his peers."

"Good to know."

"What's your gut say?"

As much as I wanted this to be an open-and-shut case, I answered, "That the husband didn't do it."

"Remember the basics. Motive, means, opportunity."

"The problem is, there are far too many people with a motive."

"Then focus on the other two."

After we hung up, I considered his comment. I didn't know the cause of death, so opportunity was my best bet. Although I wanted to pour myself a generous glass of wine and relax, the urge to solve the case prevailed. Time to pay another visit to Duncan's home. Surveillance sometimes paid off.

Brad returned from his run drenched in sweat. Duke woke up from his slumber and rushed to greet him.

"Why don't you take a quick shower, and then let's drive over to Duncan's house."

"How come?"

"He's the main suspect, and I don't have a feel for the guy other than what people have said about him. I'd like to observe him for a bit."

"Alright. Give me ten."

***

Brad parked the vehicle across the street, and I geared up the audio amplifier. After an uneventful half hour, Duncan emerged carrying a box full of what looked like liquor bottles to the trash cans. I zoomed in with the camera and snapped a picture.

In the neighboring yard, a man watered a row of boxwood bushes. When he spotted Duncan, he turned off the hose and strode toward him. "Damn, son. Dat's a lot of alcohol," he said with a twang. "You tossing it?"

"Yeah, Kenny. I'm done. No reason to drown myself in that stuff now that Madeleine's gone."

"I was real sorry to hear that she passed. Must be terrible for you."

I zoomed in closer with the camera as he patted Duncan's arm. The neighbor resembled Willie Nelson.

Duncan set the box on the driveway. "Thanks, but honestly I'm glad she's gone."

"Son, you can't mean that."

Since Duke didn't yip, I was confident that he did.

"C'mon, Kenny. You know she made my life and a lot of other people's lives miserable. All I felt was relief when I heard she was dead. And then I realized how much of my life I'd wasted."

He lifted the lid off the trash can and heaved the box inside. The sound of shattering glass vibrated in the air. After the noise died down, he continued, "Plus, the chief of police just called and informed me that her death is now a murder investigation. He wants me at the station tomorrow morning, and I need to be completely sober." Duncan dusted off his hands.

"That sounds like a wise choice." Kenny looked longingly at the trashed bottles before he said goodbye and headed back to his watering chores.

As dinnertime approached, a couple of women dropped by with casseroles. When they offered their condolences, not a single tear drifted down Duncan's cheeks, and his responses were a clipped, mechanical, "Thanks."

The activity died down, and we decided to call it a day. As Brad drove into the park, the setting sun cast hues of salmon-pink, lavender, and apricot across the sky.

He parked the vehicle at our campsite. "What do you say we order a pizza?"

"Sounds good. It's been a long day." I unbuckled my seatbelt, kissed his cheek, and then rose to pour a glass of scotch for Brad and a generous glass of wine for me.

Brad phoned in the order, fastened Duke's leash to his collar, and then stepped outside to start the campfire. I followed with our drinks.

After Brad lit the fire, I handed him his scotch. I sat in my lawn chair and watched the flames flicker. Brad settled in the chair next to me.

"How are you?" I asked.

He stared at his drink. "I keep thinking about my sister and what kind of person she would've been if she'd lived. Kristin was kind and thoughtful. On one of our trips to the park, she rescued a baby bird that had fallen out of its nest. She wanted to be a veterinarian when she grew up. She loved animals."

"I wish I could've met her."

"Yeah. Me too." He took a sip of his scotch.

Duke sat next to Brad and placed his head on his lap. "It just doesn't seem right that someone who had so much to give to the world should be taken away like that."

"Tell me more about her."

"She was a little fish. I went to all her swim meets. Breaststroke was her best, and after an all-day event, my voice would be hoarse from cheering her on." His voice broke, and his eyes misted over with tears. "Whenever she won a meet, she'd run over and give me, Mom, and Dad a high five. It's so ironic that she hit her head on the side of our pool and drowned while practicing."

Duke licked Brad's hand, and I rubbed his shoulder while he regained his composure.

"One Christmas—I think she was five." He thought for a moment. "Yeah, that'd be about right. Santa brought her a kitten, an orange tabby." Brad stared into the distance while he stroked Duke's head. "Kristin named him Charlie. She used to wrap him in bandages while she pretended to be a vet. Poor Charlie." Brad laughed and then frowned. "I swear that cat mourned her death as much as we did. He'd dart around the house searching for Kristin and then mewl when he couldn't find her."

The delivery driver interrupted our conversation with the arrival of our pizza. Duke tugged on his leash at the smell of pepperoni.

Over dinner, Brad shared more stories of holiday celebrations, neighborhood parties, and school events.

By the end of the evening, I felt like I knew both Kristin and his family better. Tonight, I'd sleep in the tent. I wasn't about to leave Brad alone after today's traumatic events.

As I snuggled up next to him in the sleeping bag, I thought about the questions I wanted to ask the tenants tomorrow. In the distance, an owl hooted, and crickets chirped. Brad's breathing slowed, and his chest rose and fell. Before long, I drifted off to sleep beside him.

At around two in the morning, a sharp cry shattered the silence.

Brad started screaming, "Help!" over and over as he tossed and turned in the sleeping bag.

Duke whined. My heart pounded as I gently shook Brad awake. He often had nightmares about his sister's drowning. This wasn't the first time I'd witnessed it.

Brad sat upright and wiped sweat off his brow with the back of his hand.

"Bad dream?"

"Yeah."

Duke pawed Brad's leg, and I heard a crack of thunder in the distance. Seconds later, the wind howled, and rain gushed over our tent.

As the canvas shook, our dog whimpered.

Brad said, "Let's make a dash for it." He grabbed the van's keys, unlocked the vehicle, then unzipped the tent.

The three of us sprinted inside while thunder rumbled, and lightning flashed across the sky. We were drenched, and pools of water formed on the van's floor.

"That's some storm." I toweled off while Brad dried Duke.

"Yeah. I didn't see that one coming. There wasn't supposed to be any rain in the forecast, but I didn't check today's weather report."

I changed into dry clothes and attempted to clean up the mess on the floor. The van smelled like a wet dog. I peered out the window to watch the light show outside. When a crack of lightning illuminated our tent, I smiled—it was toast—there'd be no more sleeping outside.

Chapter 8

When the sun came up, we assessed the damage. Leaves and branches littered the muddy ground, and our lawn chairs had tipped over. Although our cooler and camp stove remained intact, a tree limb had pierced the center of our tent. The winds had shredded the canvas, and the bedding was soaked. I spread last night's wet clothes and sleeping bags across the picnic table to dry.

We'd need to wait at least an hour for the park roads to dry out before driving to Sumter. My phone rang, and I glanced at the display. "Hi, Pete."

"You folks OK?"

"Yeah, but our tent's a goner."

"That storm was a doozy. Clayton just called from the police station. Told me to pass along the latest news to you."

It seemed the chief preferred to relay updates through Pete instead of speaking directly to me—not that I minded. I liked Pete.

"Any new developments?"

"Duncan insists he didn't kill her. Last time he saw her, she was leaving for the Piggly Wiggly on the west side of town. A friend was supposed to meet her in the parking lot and then drive her to their house for a sushi dinner. He didn't know who the friend was—or if it was a man or woman. Duncan assumed woman."

"Why not just drive herself?"

"I dunno, and neither did Duncan. Maybe she didn't want anyone to see her car parked at their house."

"Has someone checked to see if the vehicle is still in the lot?"

"Clayton was on his way when he called. Was gonna review the Piggly Wiggly's security camera footage too."

"Sounds promising." I prayed this would be the big break, and the case would be solved soon.

"Cops also discovered a couple of charges on her credit card for that day. One from the Southern Belle Boutique on Main Street and another from the Piggly Wiggly."

"Thanks. Keep me posted."

"Will do."

I glanced at my tennis shoes. Mud caked the sides. My cell lit up with a message.

Linda: Where are you? I thought you were coming home yesterday.

Me: I'm investigating a murder.

Linda: Oh no! Are you and Brad OK, Luv?

Me: Yeah. We're fine. But I'm not a happy camper.

Linda: Lol. Can I do anything for you? Check your mail?

Me: No thanks. We should be home by the end of the week.

After wiping off Duke's muddy paws, I shed my wrecked shoes and took a hot shower. Brad joined me, and we made love, easing the tension from this morning's frustrations. With a fresh attitude and a renewed sense of determination, I changed into a lime green *cabi* shirt and a pair of black shorts. I spritzed my neck with Amazing Grace and then pumped a few squirts into the van to cover any remaining wet dog smells.

The roads were muddy, but drivable, and Brad was unusually quiet as he drove to Pecan Creek Grille. I worried about how deeply the discovery of the dead body in the lake had affected him. I reached over and caressed his arm. "How are you doing?"

He grimaced. "I just wish the nightmares would stop. I hate seeing my sister in the pool and hearing my mom screaming over and over in my sleep."

"I'm sorry. Is there anything I can do?"

"No. Just having you by my side helps. I love you, Liz Adams O'Connor."

I kissed his cheek. "I love you, too."

In the backseat, Duke howled his own version of 'I love you,' and we both laughed.

When we arrived at the restaurant, a long line wound outside the door and down the sidewalk. Brad searched several minutes for a parking spot before finally giving up and parking on a side street.

"Is today a holiday?"

"Not that I know of," Brad said.

"Why are so many people here on a Monday?"

I googled May holidays on my phone. Although today wasn't a holiday, Mother's Day was less than two weeks away. I made a mental note to buy my mom a gift. Since I was an only child, Mom would never let me live it down if I forgot.

The crowd consisted mostly of women in their thirties and forties, dressed in jeans, shorts, or workout gear. We joined the back of the line.

In front of me, a woman with a sleek auburn bob leaned in and whispered to her friend, "Do you think someone killed her?"

"Hell, yeah. I just wish it'd been me. Just kidding." The blonde laughed. "Did you hear about what she did to Agnes?" She tucked a stray lock of hair behind her listening ear.

"Agnes, the sweet old lady at the end of Madeleine's street?"

"Yep. Agnes's son typically cuts her grass, but he got sick and couldn't do it for a few weeks. Madeleine reported her to the Homeowners Association."

I leaned closer as the line inched forward.

"That's terrible." The blonde crossed her arms. "Agnes is such a dear. I would've gotten Bill to cut the grass for her."

"Well, your husband's a good guy. Everyone knows Duncan's useless." Auburn bob placed her hand on her friend's shoulder. "I bet he killed her. Heard they were taking him to the station this morning."

"Do you know how she died? Did she drown?"

A woman in black Lycra yoga pants and a rainbow-colored T-shirt emblazoned with the word "Zumba" turned around and whispered, "My aunt works dispatch for the Sumter police. You didn't hear it from me, but she said Madeleine was dead before she entered the water. No gunshot wounds or obvious injuries."

The woman closest to me said, "Good to know."

All around, the air buzzed with Madeleine's name and speculation about her death. While Brad waited in line, I took Duke to the patio to find a table.

We lingered near the wrought iron gate in the back, out of the way of servers as they weaved through the crowd balancing trays of food. Sweat formed at the base of my neck. The sun blazed overhead, and the lingering humidity from last night's storm was oppressive.

After about ten minutes, a couple stood, and I scrambled to claim their seats.

Brad joined us and placed a metal stand holding a laminated number onto the table, along with a coffee for himself and an iced tea for me. I rose to fetch a bowl of water and a treat for Duke.

While our dog gobbled his biscuit, Brad said, "I wonder how long it will take to get our food. I'm starving."

My stomach grumbled a loud response, and I laughed. "I guess I'm hungry too. I feel sorry for Chief Clayton and for whoever prosecutes the culprit when they're caught."

"Why?"

"Did you hear those women in line in front of us? It will be tough to find a jury that's not tainted."

Brad scrolled through his phone while I people-watched. Twenty minutes later, Brock emerged with a tray of food. "Who got the omelet?"

I raised my hand.

"Alright, a spinach and mushroom omelet for the lady and the scrambled special for the gentleman." He glanced at Duke. "I remember you guys. Aren't you staying at Poinsett Park?"

"Yes. We planned on leaving yesterday, but then Brad discovered Madeleine's body in the lake."

Brock extracted a handkerchief from the pocket of his apron and wiped his brow with it. "You're the one who found our landlady?"

Brad cringed and then set the forkful of eggs back on his plate. "Yeah." He picked up his mug and took a sip of coffee.

"That must've been troubling. Mind if I sit? It's been a crazy morning, and I'd like to hear your side of the story versus all the speculation."

Brad nodded.

"Are you sure?" I don't want to interrupt your breakfast." He pointed at Brad's untouched eggs.

"Please join us. The more I talk about it, the less surreal it seems."

Brock took the seat across from Brad and slipped Duke a treat. Our dog rewarded him with a lick on the hand.

I swallowed a forkful of fluffy egg oozing with cheddar, mushrooms, and spinach while Brad gave a brief description of that morning. When he finished, he finally took a bite of his meal.

"Are the cops making you guys stay in town?" Brock asked.

I glanced at Brad's full mouth and then answered Brock's question. "No, we can leave anytime we want. We just felt like it was the right thing to do to stick around a few more days." I paused and then asked, "The other day, you mentioned that all the tenants were united in their hatred for Madeleine. Do you think one of them killed her?"

He shrugged. "I suppose it's possible, but my money's on Duncan." He motioned across the patio. "According to gossip central, time of death was around nine p.m., so I can tell you four of us who didn't do it."

I peppered my hashbrowns while Brock explained. "Last night, Ruth, Joy, Stacey, and I, along with about fifteen other people went out to dinner to celebrate Ruth's birthday. We shut the place down at midnight."

Duke didn't yip, and I did a fist pump under the table. Four suspects had just been knocked off the list.

Brock left, and Brad mopped up the last tidbits of scrambled eggs off his plate with a piece of whole wheat toast. "What's next?"

"Dang, you inhaled your breakfast. Give me a few minutes and then let's visit Michelle and DZ. I'll see if she has time to give me lash extensions." I wondered if the barber shop would be just as packed.

When we entered Southern Scissors, every booth was full. DZ waved at us from his station. "Howdy, folks. What can I do for you?"

"I'd like to get lash extensions if Michelle has the time."

"She's in the back with a client. Have a seat."

If Pecan Creek Grille was the epicenter for the women of Sumter, Southern Scissors was the gathering place for retired men.

"C'mon, DZ. I know you did it. Knocked that wench off didn't ya?" DZ's client chuckled. The stout older gentleman's body filled the chair.

Unfazed, DZ continued to trim the man's beard. "Wasn't me or my wife." He chuckled. "Our alibi is airtight." He waggled a finger in the air. "Last night, we hosted a barbecue for a few of our neighbors. They'll attest to it." DZ paused to examine his work and then continued to snip. "Word on the street is Duncan did it."

No yip from Duke.

In a booth across from DZ, a woman trimmed the long gray tresses of a man's hair. A monarch butterfly tattoo sprawled across her upper left arm. I recognized the man in the chair as Duncan's neighbor Kenny.

"Talked to that boy yesterday. He tossed out all his liquor. Said he was gonna get sober."

"You serious, Kenny?" DZ's client asked.

"Dang straight."

"We'll see how long that lasts," the stout man replied.

While the men continued to speculate about who murdered Madeleine, I tugged Brad's sleeve. "Let's go." I waved goodbye to DZ. "Be back later."

No need for lash extensions now. I'd just scratched two more suspects off the list.

Once we were outside, I lavished love on Duke, my canine lie detector. "You are the best boy," I said as I scratched his back. Duke wiggled his body and wagged his tail in response. "Let's check out the boutique Madeleine visited, and then we'll stop by the tavern. Racheal owes me an order of Tipsy bites."

Brad slipped Duke a treat. "OK."

A large black-and-white striped awning with the words Southern Belle inscribed in fuchsia hung over the glass entrance. Duke and Brad remained in the van.

When I stepped into the store, I was immediately drawn to a rack of colorful blouses. As I flipped through the hangers, a woman in her mid-forties approached me. She was dressed in a floral-print A-line dress, and her platinum hair was swept back in an elegant bun. "How may I help you?"

"I'm looking for a fun top to wear to a friend's birthday." By serendipity, my hand landed on the exact same green-and-pink blouse that Madeleine wore when Brad discovered her body. "Oh, this is perfect."

The woman gasped, and her eyes watered. "I'm sorry," she sniffled. "Our best customer just passed away. She bought that blouse yesterday."

I eyed the price tag: $278. Madeleine had a high cost per wear on that one. "How awful. I'm so sorry. What happened?"

The shopkeeper continued, "They found her body in a nearby lake. They're saying she was murdered."

I fished some tissues out of my purse and handed them to her.

"Madeleine left wearing that top. She was headed to a friend's house for dinner." She dabbed her eyes.

"Did she mention her friend's name?"

She gave me a funny look. "Why do you ask?"

"Sorry. I'm curious by nature. None of my business."

"That's OK. She never mentioned a name."

"But she did say it was a woman?"

"I believe Madeleine said she. Although I guess she could've said he." She took a deep breath and then asked, "Do you want to try that on?"

"Sure." I randomly grabbed a couple more blouses and followed her to the dressing rooms. One hundred and fifty dollars later, I rejoined Brad and Duke in the van. I couldn't bring myself to buy the same top as the dead woman wore, but I did score a lovely leopard-print blouse.

Despite the scorching midday sun, the patio of Tipsy Tavern buzzed with activity, and once again we had trouble finding a seat. The fans worked overtime, and every umbrella was open. The early May temperatures were unseasonably warm. I spotted Ruth from the insurance agency at a table by herself with her dog, Maggie. She waved and motioned for us to join her. Maggie's whole body quivered with delight as she greeted Duke.

"You're not working today?" I asked.

"No. Joy gave us the rest of the day off. The place was dead this morning." Ruth gave an awkward laugh. "I guess that wasn't the best choice of words." She paused and then explained. "Everyone's too busy gossiping about our landlady's death. The last thing on their minds is conducting any kind of normal business."

"Thanks for sharing your table. We had breakfast at Pecan Creek Grille this morning. The place buzzed with locals talking about the murder." I extended my hand. "By the way, I'm Liz, and this is Brad. Happy belated birthday."

"Thank you." Ruth accepted the gesture. "How'd you know it was my birthday?"

Brad chimed in, "Brock mentioned last night's party."

Our conversation was interrupted when Racheal appeared.

"You folks know what you want?" She flipped the pad of paper to a new page and clicked the top of the pen with her left hand.

Since I was still full after our breakfast, I ordered the Greek salad. Ruth asked for the turkey club, and Brad ordered a cheeseburger.

"Kitchen's a little backed up, so could be a bit of a wait."

"No problem," Brad said.

"And don't worry, Liz. I added those Tipsy bites that I owe you to your order."

Racheal left, and Ruth speculated on who might have murdered Madeleine. "I doubt that Duncan did it."

"Why?" I asked.

She numbered off the reasons with her fingers. "Well, for one, he was probably drunk that night. For two, I don't believe he'd have the backbone to do something like that. Look what he put up with for years. For three, from what I've heard, whoever did it was clever. No gun, no visible wounds. Made to look like a drowning. That doesn't sound like Duncan's style to me."

"Well, if not him, then who do you think killed her?" Brad asked.

Ruth leaned forward. "I bet she had a boyfriend. Madeleine was a woman who craved attention, and she wasn't getting it from her husband. Who knows, maybe the boyfriend was married, and the wife found out."

So far, Duke hadn't yipped once, even though everything Ruth said was conjecture.

"What about the other tenants?"

She shook her head. "We all had our reasons to hate her, but murder her? If anyone in the center killed her, I'd be shocked. I've known some of these people for years. I just don't see it."

I seized the opportunity to get Ruth's perspective on the others. "How well do you know Sherry?"

"She kind of keeps to herself, but she does have her car insurance through us." Ruth leaned over and placed her hand on my arm. "Have you ever had her do a tarot reading for you?"

I nodded.

"Sherry's creepy accurate. A couple of years ago, I was in the market for a house. As a result of the reading, I ended up buying my second choice, which was the best decision I've ever made. Not only am I around the corner from a dog park, but it also turned out that the other one would have been a money pit."

While Ruth continued to provide background on the other tenants, clouds drifted overhead and provided some relief from the heat. By the time our lunch arrived, the outdoor crowd had started to thin.

Racheal set the tray on the table and served our food. "I can't believe the sales we had today. I bet we get a night crowd too. This might even top St. Paddy's Day."

After she placed the Tipsy bites in front of me, I asked, "Did you turn that notebook over to the cops?"

"Of course."

Duke yipped.

"What notebook?" Ruth asked.

"Racheal has a log of all of Madeleine's wrongdoings as a landlady."

"Must be a thick book," Ruth commented. "Hey, are you and Sherry still having your true crime nights? I might want to join you for the next one."

"Yep, every Monday at seven, unless I have to work. Next one is at my house. Um, can I get you anything else? It's still super busy in there."

"All good," Brad said.

"What's a true crime night?" I asked Ruth after Racheal left.

"They get together and cook dinner while they watch *48 Hours*. Racheal and Robert live just down the street from Sherry. Might be a little wine involved too." Ruth winked.

As we wrapped up lunch, my phone pinged with a text message from Pete.

Pete: Where are you?

Me: Sumter. Just finished eating lunch.

Pete: I have news on the case. Can you stop by on your way back? I'd rather tell you in person.

Me: Be right there.

Chapter 9

Brad sped down the highway leading to Poinsett Park. Duke jumped out as soon as we arrived at the ranger station and rushed inside to greet his friend.

"Well, hello, fella." Pete bent over and patted Duke's head.

"Sorry. I didn't get a chance to snap his leash to his collar. Guess he was excited to see you." I fastened the leather strap to the metal ring while Duke's tail swished in the air. "What's the big news?"

Pete nodded his approval. "Appreciate you following the rules. Clayton stopped by 'bout an hour ago. Toxicology results are back. Someone poisoned her. Some kind of toxic mushroom."

"Wow." That confirmed my suspicion that the person she had dinner with was responsible. "Any idea what kind?"

"Not yet. Lab's working on it."

"What else did they find in her stomach?"

"Sushi rolls. Salad. No other poisons." He tugged at his mustache. "There's more. Cops found a garbage bag containing damp clothes and a king-sized sheet on a deserted road five miles from the park. The clothes were black, men's large. Might be unrelated, but it's suspicious."

"Any cameras nearby?"

"Nah. It's pretty remote. The lab's trying to recover any DNA. Slim chance with the heat and humidity. They're also testing water samples—might match the lake."

If the clothing belonged to the killer, that ruled out tiny Racheal. "Anything else?" I asked.

"Clayton dropped off a copy of the evidence log." Pete handed me a form. "It includes the contents in her purse."

"Thanks." I folded the paper and tucked it into my pocket.

When we arrived back at the van, Brad poured two glasses of shiraz and then began to prep dinner in the van's small kitchen. The monotony of the tasks seemed to soothe his nerves. After I folded up the now-dry bedding, I faced the whiteboard. Duke hung out with Brad near the food.

I uncapped the marker and scratched through Ruth, Joy, DZ, Michelle, Brock, and Stacey. Under "Knowns," I added *Method: poisonous mushroom.* Under "Questions," I penned *Are the clothes and the sheet relevant, and where were they discovered? Where were the mushrooms sourced?* If the clothing belonged to the killer, then the murderer might be a man. But that was in contradiction to what the shopkeeper had relayed about who Madeleine had dinner with that night. Next, I added *Does Madeleine have a boyfriend?*

I placed a call to Pete's cell.

He answered immediately and asked, "Everything OK?"

"We're fine. I was just wondering—is it possible that Madeleine was having an affair?"

"Highly unlikely. Her grandfather was notorious for cheating on her grandmother. Maddie had very strong opinions against it."

Hmm, maybe. But sometimes the apple didn't fall far from the tree.

"Where's the area where the clothes were found?" I asked.

Pete said, "I'll text the directions to you."

My phone pinged with a response, and I looked up the road on Google Maps. Although it was doubtful there were any clues yet to be uncovered at the site, I added a visit to my to-do list.

While I sipped my wine, I unfolded the evidence log and reviewed the contents found in Madeleine's Gucci handbag: a large makeup bag with cosmetics, a mirror, pens, a notepad, a pair of sunglasses, a receipt from the Piggly Wiggly, a pillbox with vitamins, tissues, her cell phone, a key ring, a matching Gucci wallet, a small pink notebook with a list of to do's, and a business card holder.

Although everything had been soaked, the person who compiled the log had been meticulous, documenting the purse's contents in detail and assigning each item an evidence number. The phone had been bagged and flagged for forensic analysis. As best they could, they'd recorded the items on the to-do list, itemized two dozen business cards, and included any relevant notes.

The numbered tasks included *Get lashes done, Buy a new outfit, Pick up flowers and wine*, along with a series of business-related actions. According to the information on the form, the grocery store receipt was harder to decipher, but it appeared to be for a bouquet of flowers and a bottle of wine.

Why would Madeleine buy flowers for a man? And could the murderer have worn men's clothing to throw off the investigation, knowing the garbage bag might be found?

The list of business cards included a card for each of the center's tenants. Scrawled on the back of The Cat's Meow's card was the number seven. Some of Sherry's tarot cards had numbers on them, and I wondered if the note was associated with a reading. Jotted on the card for Tipsy Tavern were the words "David—catering."

David, Racheal's father. I'd forgotten to list the cook as a suspect. He'd be familiar with mushrooms. Maybe he had murdered Madeleine to put an end to his daughter's obsession. I added his name under "Suspects." As I took another sip of the shiraz, I remembered the Asian cookbook Racheal had thumbed through at the Tavern.

I made a note to visit the Piggly Wiggly to see if anyone recalled Madeleine's visit that fateful evening. I was getting closer. I could feel it in my bones. I transferred my wine to a plastic cup and joined Brad outside.

Brad placed chicken, shrimp, and veggie kabobs coated in barbecue sauce onto the campfire grate. Embers sparked, and I inhaled the smell of hickory smoke. While Duke snored softly next to my chair, I queued up Sarah McLachlan's "Building a Mystery" on my phone.

"Does my favorite sleuth have any new theories?"

"I added David to the suspect list."

"Who?" He added foil-wrapped corn to the fire.

"David—he's the cook for Tipsy Tavern and Racheal's dad." I listed the reasons. "The cause of death was poisonous mushrooms. His daughter had an unhealthy obsession with Madeleine's wrongdoings." I held up one finger and then another. "Method and motive."

"Sounds plausible."

The more I considered the possibility, the stronger I felt about David as a suspect. "He could've easily carried her body into the lake. And maybe those were his clothes they found."

"It's a solid theory. Do you know if he has a history of violence?"

"No, and I don't know where he was at the time of the murder. But it's at the top of my list to find out. Tomorrow, let's check out that road and see if the cops overlooked anything."

"Alright." He flipped the skewers and poked open a foil packet. "About ten more minutes."

My mouth watered in response.

After dinner, Brad leaned in and winked. "How about dessert in the van?" He stood and gave me one of his toe-tingling kisses, then grabbed my hand and pulled me toward the vehicle. Once inside, I handed Duke a rawhide to occupy him while Brad and I enjoyed the comfort of the van's bed.

Around two in the morning, Brad began yelling, "Help! Hurry!" I gently shook him awake, and he sat upright while his breathing slowly returned to normal. A few minutes later, we heard scratching sounds outside the van.

My heart dropped. Thieves, *again*? I grabbed my gun and a couple of flashlights and then stepped outside, only to discover thieves of an entirely different species.

A pack of raccoons gathered around the remnants of last night's meal. Brad and I doubled over in laughter as Duke and the coons had a standoff. While our dog barked and whined, the raccoons stood on their hind legs and hissed. After an intense minute, the creatures lumbered off toward the lake.

Duke trotted back toward us, proud of his victory. "Good boy," I said before we retreated into the van.

***

I peeled back the covers and tiptoed into the kitchen, careful not to wake Brad and Duke. After I brewed a cup of English tea laced with milk and honey, I slipped outside to watch the sunrise. Steam hovered over the lake as hues of apricot, burnt orange, and pink lit up the sky. Despite last night's lack of sleep, I felt energized for the day.

Today's agenda included a visit to Piggly Wiggly, Tipsy Tavern, and The Cat's Meow. The spot where the garbage bag had been dumped was on the way.

There'd likely be loose ends to tie up, but I was confident that I'd be able to point the cops toward the culprit. If all went well, we'd be back in Charleston by tomorrow.

My phone pinged with a text.

Linda: How's it going, Luv?

Me: Good. On track to be home by the end of the week.

Linda: Great. Let's celebrate over a glass of wine. We can plan our next neighborhood gathering.

I sent her a thumbs-up.

An hour later, a sleepy Brad emerged with a mug of coffee.

"Where's Duke?" I asked.

"Still sleeping. Guess the coons wore him out." He plopped into the chair beside me. "So, what's my favorite detective got planned for today?"

"I thought we'd check out the dump site and then head to the Piggly Wiggly and ask the staff if they remember anything about Madeleine's visit that day."

"OK." He yawned and took a long sip of the caffeinated brew.

"After that, we'll stop by the Cat's Meow and Tipsy Tavern to determine who had an alibi for that night... and who didn't." I rubbed my hands together in anticipation.

"Sounds good." He set the mug on the ground and stretched his arms toward the sky. "Mind if I get a run in first?"

"Not at all. Taking Duke?"

"Yeah, I think I will this time."

***

As we drove down the dirt road, I noticed the absence of streetlights. The area would be pitch black at night. "Let's park the car and walk." The road was a mile and a half long and dead-ended at Poinsett's perimeter fence.

I snapped Duke's leash to his collar and said, "Duke, find." Our dog put his nose to the ground. Right before the street ended, he tugged on the leash and led us into the woods on the other side of the road. Stems of faded pink roses were tossed out of sight beneath a tree.

I pulled a plastic bag out of my pocket. Bending down, I gingerly picked up half a dozen faded pink roses and placed them in the bag.

"Clue?"

"Maybe. I don't know why flowers would be tossed out in the boondocks. Madeleine bought a bouquet before she went to dinner at her friend's house. After we stop by the grocery store, let's drop this off at the police station."

Brad and Duke waited in the van, while I stepped through the sliding glass doors and strode toward the wine section.

A man in a Piggly Wiggly T-shirt restocked the shelves. His nametag identified him as Manny - Manager of Wine, Spirits, and Beer.

"How can I help you?" he asked.

I handed him my business card. "I'm helping with the investigation into Madeleine Collins's death. Were you working last Saturday?"

Manny studied the card and slipped it into his pocket. "Yeah, I was here. Already told the cops everything I remembered, but I guess I can go over it again." He turned back toward the shelf and straightened a row of bottles. "She asked me for a wine recommendation—something to pair with sushi. I recommended a mid-priced sauvignon blanc, but she insisted on something more expensive."

"Did she say why?"

"Said she was having dinner at a friend's house and wanted to impress her."

"Are you sure she said *her*?"

"Positive."

"What else did she say?"

"Nothing. Not even a thank you."

"I appreciate your time. If anything else comes to mind, will you call me?"

"Of course." Manny bent down, pulled two wine bottles from a box, and placed them on the shelf.

As I approached the floral department, I admired the kaleidoscope of colors. Bins overflowed with sunflowers, roses, carnations, and lilies. Potted plants and multihued arrangements perched atop wooden crates. Behind the counter, a woman tucked greenery into a vase filled with gerbera daisies. Her nametag read Ashley - Floral Clerk.

I handed her my business card and repeated the spiel I'd given to Manny. "Did you work last Saturday?"

"No. I only work during the week while my kids are in school."

"How many kids do you have?"

"Three. Two girls and a boy. All under the age of eleven."

"Wow, that must be tough trying to balance your job and raise your kids."

"Yeah. Some days I wonder how I do it." She tucked the last piece of fern into the cylinder glass container.

I gestured toward the arrangement. "That's beautiful."

She smiled. "Thanks."

"Do you know who did work on that day?"

"My friend Jennifer." She glanced at her phone. "She should be out of class right now. Do you want me to call her?"

"Yes, please."

"Hey, Jen. There's a private investigator here asking questions about that woman who was murdered. Her name's Liz. She wants to talk to you." Ashley handed me the phone.

Jennifer sighed. "I already told the police everything I know."

"I understand, but I'd appreciate hearing it firsthand."

"Fine. I worked that day. Madeleine asked for flowers that matched the pink in her blouse."

"Did she say who they were for?"

"Nope, and I didn't ask."

After I thanked her, I handed the phone back to Ashley and quickly returned to the van.

"Well, that blows my theory about David." I fastened my seatbelt. "The wine manager is positive that the person Madeleine was having dinner with was a *she*."

Chapter 10

Although both the chief and I had doubted the relevance of the found roses, Madeleine's request for flowers that matched her blouse lent more credence to the clue. He thanked me for my efforts.

When we arrived at The Cat's Meow, the shop bustled with customers. I waved at Sherry, and her cat, Jazz, leapt off the counter and trotted over to greet Duke.

After I selected a spiral rose-gold metal wind chime for my mom, Brad and I wove through the crowd toward the checkout. As we passed the patrons, I caught snippets of conversation.

"Were you able to book a reading?" a tall, slender woman asked as she browsed a carousel of greeting cards.

"Yeah, but not until next Tuesday." The short, stocky female next to her held up a T-shirt with the Superwoman logo. "This is cute."

"Mine's tomorrow. I'll let you know how it goes."

When we reached the register, I smiled at Sherry. "You're busy."

"Yeah. No one's buying any merchandise but look at this." She held up a calendar filled with appointments. "Nothing like a sudden death to make people wonder what the future holds." She glanced at Brad and grinned. "So, who's this handsome guy?"

After I introduced them, Gypsy poked her head out from behind the counter. When she spotted Duke, she purred. Sherry placed her palm on the top of Brad's hand. Her eyes twinkled. "I'd love to do a tarot reading for you."

"Umm... no thanks."

I nudged him under the counter. A reading would be a great opportunity to gather information from Sherry without other distractions.

He cleared his throat. "On second thought, sure, I'll give it a try."

"Can you be here at eight-thirty tomorrow morning? I'll open the store early just for you."

After penning Brad's name in, she passed him a business card with the appointment time.

"Everyone seems to be speculating about your landlady's death." I handed Sherry the wind chime and my credit card. "What were you doing the night of her murder?"

"Well, that's an odd question." She scanned the price, swiped the card, and slipped the purchase into a bag with the shop's logo. "I was home."

"Alone?"

She pointed at her cats. "With these two, I'm never alone." Without another word, she passed the bag to me and turned to help the next customer.

Duke didn't yip, but her answer was evasive.

As we left the store and walked toward Tipsy Tavern, Brad asked, "Um, why am I getting a reading?"

"At the beginning of the session, she'll tell you to silently think of a question. We'll craft one that's specific to the case."

He paused mid-step. "You don't believe in that stuff, do you?"

"Of course not, but Sherry will be more relaxed and open. She may say things that she wouldn't otherwise share."

When we reached the back patio, I smiled at our good fortune. David, Racheal's dad and the tavern's chef, worked a crossword puzzle at a nearby table. We took the spot next to him.

"Nice dog. What's his name?" David asked.

"Duke." Brad extended his hand. "I'm Brad, and this is Liz."

"I've already met Liz. I'm David. If you're looking for food, kitchen doesn't officially open until eleven."

Robert approached with a notepad in hand and clicked his pen. "What can I get you folks to drink? Bloody Mary? Mimosa?"

"I'll take a virgin Bloody Mary," Brad said.

"You'll love it. We load it with vegetables. And for you, Liz?"

"An iced tea—"

"With a splash of sweet. Got it." Robert grinned. "Be right back."

David tapped his pencil on the newspaper. "What's a nine-letter word for puzzle? Starts with a 'C.'"

"Conundrum," I said without hesitation.

"Thanks." He turned toward Brad. "Hey, you're the guy who found the body."

"Yeah. That's me."

"That had to be upsetting."

Brad closed his eyes and nodded.

My heart squeezed at Brad's reaction to David's comment. "Did you see Madeleine on the day she died?"

"Nope. Racheal talked to her briefly. She said Madeleine wasn't her usual grumpy self. I was holed up in the kitchen from eleven in the morning to ten that night. We were short-staffed."

Not a single yip from Duke.

Robert returned with our drinks. He half-smiled before he said, "To-day when I was at the bank, an old lady asked me to check her balance..." He paused for effect. "So, I pushed her over."

He chuckled as he set the iced tea in front of me and then handed Brad a glass of spicy tomato juice with skewers of olives, cucumbers, cherry tomatoes, and pickled carrots, topped off with a crisp celery stalk.

Once I'd recovered from his latest dad joke, I said, "Wow, that's a meal by itself."

While I sipped my tea, I sorted the puzzle pieces of Madeleine's death in my mind. Who among the remaining suspects had the opportunity? Duncan claimed he was passed out on their couch all night. Although everyone else believed he was the culprit, my gut said he wasn't, even though he didn't have an alibi.

I needed to determine where Robert and Racheal were the evening of her murder. Had they colluded to get rid of their landlady?

"Who else worked that night?" I asked David.

"Me, Racheal, and Robert. Robert and I closed. Racheal left around ten." David glanced at his watch and folded his newspaper. "Thanks for the help with the crossword puzzle. I better get back to the kitchen. Enjoy your drinks."

No yip from Duke. The list of suspects was narrowing.

My phone pinged with a text from Pete.

Pete: DNA results from the clothes, the sheet in the garbage bag, and the roses you dropped off should be back by tomorrow.

Me: Fast turnaround on the flowers. Great news.

Pete: Techs had no luck retrieving the data from Madeleine's cell phone, but Clayton said they finally got the records from her cell phone provider. You want a copy?

Me: Yes.

Pete: OK. I'll let the chief know.

As Brad paid our bill, Racheal drove up in a black Honda Civic. She lifted a couple of grocery bags out of the trunk and then waved hello before she ducked inside the bar. I fetched a Post-it out of my purse and noted the license plate on the midsize sedan.

On the way back to our campsite, we stopped at the police station to collect the printouts of her phone activity.

Once we were settled back at the park, I spread the pages across the table and searched for activity on the day of her death. An incoming text received at 6:30 p.m. caught my eye. Someone had already identified Duncan's number on my copy, and it wasn't from his phone. "Can I see that business card Sherry gave you?"

Brad handed me the card. The numbers matched.

"Looks like Madeleine was communicating with Sherry on the day she died." I recalled Sherry's sarcastic comment about the two of them getting together.

Brad stretched his arms toward the ceiling. "I'm going for a bike ride."

I sensed that he needed a break from the case. "I'm sorry this has consumed so much of my time."

"No need to apologize. I'm the one who encouraged you to take it on." He kissed my cheek. "When I get back, I'll cook us an early dinner."

"You're the best. I love you."

Duke reluctantly stayed behind with me. As I combed through the calls and texts, I highlighted any frequent contacts. I rose and returned to the whiteboard. When I added Racheal's name next to the question *Who drives a midsize sedan?*, I wondered if either car appeared on the footage from the Piggly Wiggly. Although I hadn't noted the license number on Sherry's car, I had recorded the digits on Racheal's plate.

I phoned the police chief, but the call went to voicemail. I left a message with descriptions of both vehicles and asked if he could have someone review the video footage to determine if either car was near the store that Saturday.

"Wanna go for a walk?" Duke raced to the door of the van. I jotted a quick note to Brad and then snapped the leash onto Duke's collar. Perhaps some exercise and fresh air would provide new insights into the case.

I chose one of the easier routes, Scout Trail. A gentle breeze blew through the trees, creating a soothing rustling sound. A pair of cardinals chirped as they flew overhead. We crossed a small bridge, and Duke worked his nose along the wooden planks. Up ahead, an armadillo lumbered across the path.

My phone buzzed inside my pocket, and I fished it out.

"This is Liz."

A female voice replied, "Officer Lopez here. Chief Clayton asked me to update you on our review of the footage."

That was fast. "Did you find the Civic or the Malibu?"

"Two black Hondas pulled into the Piggly Wiggly just before Madeleine. Neither matched the plate you provided, but one image is fuzzy. We did spot a dark gray Malibu with pawprint decals on the windows around 6:20 p.m. The driver wasn't visible, nor were the plates. The car moved to the far side of the lot, out of camera range, and possibly exited through the back."

"Where did Madeleine go when she left?"

"Same direction as the Malibu."

"Tell the chief I'm pretty sure that car belongs to Sherry Roma, owner of the Cat's Meow."

"Will do."

When Duke and I returned, I poured a glass of wine to celebrate the progress on the case. Brad was still out on his bike ride, so I fed our dog and started dinner. As I sliced mushrooms for the steaks, I thought about the poisonous ones that had killed Madeleine. Sherry had owned a restaurant—she might know a thing or two about mushrooms. I made a mental note to ask her. Her response and reaction could confirm my growing suspicion that she was the one who'd murdered Madeleine.

I bumped my elbow on the edge of the counter in the small space and winced at the sharp pain that radiated down my arm. Enough of this. Tomorrow, we'd bring Duke to Brad's reading and ask Sherry if she murdered the woman. The police could sort out the rest. I was ready to close this case and return to the comfort of our spacious kitchen in Charleston.

***

At 8:30 a.m. sharp, Duke, Brad, and I entered The Cat's Meow. The bells chimed overhead, announcing our arrival. Sherry emerged from the back of the shop.

"Well, hello." Sherry dusted off her hands. A warm smile spread across her face. "I was just unpacking some boxes." Her cats trotted over to greet their furry friend. While Jazz wound between Duke's legs, Gypsy purred, her tail flicking with delight.

Sherry batted her eyelashes at my husband. "So, handsome, are you ready for your reading?"

Brad nodded, and Sherry motioned him toward the counter. After her usual ritual to cleanse the space, she took a deep breath and shuffled the deck of tarot cards.

"Brad, close your eyes and ask your question. Please don't voice it out loud."

Although I didn't believe in all this hocus pocus, the first reading still haunted me. Last night, Brad and I had agreed on our approach to the session. He'd make the question very specific: *Was Sherry Roma the sole murderer of Madeleine Collins?* Although I could ask her straight up, the woman was clever. I needed her to relax before we directly broached the subject.

When Brad opened his eyes, Sherry studied his face.

"Ready?"

"Yes."

Sherry spread the deck face down and circled her hands clockwise and then counterclockwise. She stopped, withdrew a card, and placed it face-up in front of us. An image of a hand holding a branch glared back.

"The Ace of Wands. If your question was open-ended, you'll need to stay aligned with your goals and be prepared to spring into action. If you asked a yes or no question, the answer to your question is yes."

It took all I had in me not to gasp out loud. Brad glanced my way, his eyes wide.

Sherry let the answer soak in and then asked, "Shall we continue?"

Brad turned his attention back to Sherry. "Sure."

She flipped over an image of an upside-down woman enclosed in an ellipse of leaves. "Ah, The World... reversed. You should be careful what you ask for. Although you may have success, you will likely get less than what you expected." She suggested that Brad reflect on the reading after the session.

"Last card." For a third time, she performed the same routine with her palms. She paused and repeated the ritual before she settled on a card. "Another reversal."

I stared at the picture captioned "The Magician."

Sherry rubbed her chin. "Someone may be trying to deceive you. It's also possible that your goals are not aligned with the highest good."

Duke whined, and the cats snuggled closer to him.

Brad gave me a puzzled look, as if to say, "*Now what?*"

Sherry gathered the cards.

"Thanks for the reading." I extracted my wallet from my purse to pay for her services.

"Um, yeah. Thanks. That was enlightening," Brad added.

"My pleasure. Do you want to browse a bit before I check you out?"

I met her gaze and asked, "Did you kill Madeleine?"

"What?" Sherry's mouth dropped open. "How could you ask such a thing? Of course not."

Duke yipped, and the felines scattered.

Brad crossed his arms across his chest and glared at Sherry.

"I mean, I wasn't fond of the woman. Not many people were," she stammered, "but I didn't murder her."

Duke yipped for a second time.

"What's wrong with your dog?" Sherry asked.

"Can we pay up? I think he needs to go out."

"Of course." After she rang us up, she said, "Come back soon."

"We will." Duke yipped for the third time.

Back in the van, I breathed a sigh of relief. Brad high-fived me and then pulled me into a lingering kiss. As our lips parted, I watched the tension fade from his face. We'd identified Madeleine's murderer, and justice would be served.

I placed a call to the chief. "Sherry Roma is your murderer."

"What makes you say that?"

"It all adds up—the cell phone records, the dinner time note on the business card, the camera footage, the tire tracks, and the flowers. Even the clothing matches her frame."

A few moments of silence passed before he responded, "Circumstantial. There's no smoking gun."

"Did you get the DNA results back?"

"Yes. Madeleine's DNA was on the sheet, but anything on the flowers, clothes, or garbage bag had either been nonexistent or compromised. We'll need more concrete evidence for the DA to proceed."

"May I make a few suggestions?"

"Shoot."

"Check the cameras in Sherry's neighborhood and see if you can find her car leaving that night. Or better yet, bring her in for questioning. Maybe she'll take a lie detector test. I'm confident she's the culprit."

Hallelujah. Our camping trip was finally over.

After we packed up our gear, we drove to the ranger station to settle our bill.

Pete greeted us. "Sorry to see you folks go. Hope you'll come back real soon. If there's a trial, I'll be sure to reserve your campsite for you."

Ugh, a trial—we'd be summoned as witnesses. I pushed the thought to the back of my mind.

Pete handed me a paper bag filled with treats. "This is for my favorite junior park ranger." He opened his wallet and extracted a dollar. "And this is for you from the chief."

"Thanks." When I leaned over to hug him, he blushed. "Will you keep me posted on the investigation?"

"Sure thing." He unwrapped a Hershey's Kiss and popped it into his mouth as we waved our goodbyes.

Chapter 11

Nine Months Later

Brad and I had been summoned as witnesses in the State of South Carolina vs. Sherry Roma trial. Although Pete had reserved our campsite, we were staying at the Hamton Inn, courtesy of the prosecution. We'd left the Sprinter at home and brought Brad's SUV instead. After the hotel-provided breakfast, we dropped Duke off at a nearby doggy day care center and made the short drive to the Sumter County Courthouse.

Inside the courtroom, we found seats two rows behind the prosecuting attorney and his associates. Park Ranger Pete and Chief Clayton sat in front of us, and Pete turned to say hello.

I leaned toward him for a better view of the defense table. Amid a team of women, Sherry sat poised, wearing what appeared to be a long-sleeved navy dress. On the opposing side of the room, the jury box contained twelve men and women of varying ages and ethnicities.

"All rise for the Honorable Judge Martha Clark," the court bailiff announced.

A petite woman with shoulder-length chestnut hair, tortoiseshell glasses, and a long black robe took her place at the front of the courtroom.

"You may be seated." A buzz of activity ensued as we all silenced our cell phones per the bailiff's instructions.

Clad in a gray pinstripe suit, the prosecuting attorney rose and introduced himself as Earl Beaufort. As I listened to his opening statement, I prayed there was enough evidence to convict Sherry of first-degree murder.

After Beaufort's speech, Sherry's attorney, Ms. Charlotte Sinclair, addressed the jury. Her straw-colored pixie cut gave her an air of professionalism, and her cherry-red blazer paired with a black pencil skirt exuded confidence.

I squirmed in my seat as she listed all the reasons why the state didn't have a case.

When she finished, the judge turned her attention to Earl. "Counselor."

He stood. "Your Honor, the prosecution calls Brad O'Connor to the stand."

As my husband made his way to the front of the courtroom, I admired the way his tan suit hugged his fit body. The color matched his sandy brown hair. A few of the women in the jury box noted his good looks.

After Brad was sworn in, Earl took his time as he approached his witness. "Mr. O'Connor." He paused for effect. "Please tell the jury what happened on the morning of May 13th."

While he described the discovery of Madeleine's body in the park's lake, a young Hispanic juror placed her hand over her heart. I hoped reliving the trauma wouldn't be a catalyst for the return of nightmares about his sister's drowning. He hadn't had one since we'd left Poinsett Park.

Once the defense completed their cross-examination, Brad took his seat next to me, and I squeezed his hand. "You did great," I whispered in his ear.

A full morning of testimonies ensued before the judge called a break for lunch. Pete turned and said, "Clayton and I are walking to a deli down the street. You two want to join us?"

"Sure," Brad replied.

The four of us sat at a square wooden table in a corner away from the lunch crowd so we could discuss the trial.

"I'm glad that's over." Brad took a bite of his pastrami on wheat bread.

Before I bit into my French dip, I tucked a napkin into the front of the cream camisole I wore underneath the royal-blue blazer I'd purchased from the fall *cabi* catalog. The jacket's border matched my black pants.

"What'd you think of this morning?" I asked no one in particular.

Clayton shook his head. "Not good. Charlotte tripped up Officer Lopez a couple of times during her testimony." He tore open a bag of salt and vinegar chips. "I hope you can make up for that this afternoon."

Yikes, no pressure. I was the first witness after the break.

Pete licked a stray piece of chicken salad off his thumb. "Me too. Each time Lopez tried to link the evidence to Sherry, Charlotte would blow it out of the water. She's tough."

"I'm not sure how her approach is playing with the jurors, but I couldn't get a good read." I dipped my sandwich in the au jus. "I thought Earl did a good job."

When the chief picked up his BLT, mayonnaise oozed out the side, dripping onto the plate. "I keep asking myself, did we find enough evidence to convict Sherry?"

"Your team did a great job. You did everything you could to uncover the truth." If Duke were around, would he have yipped?

Why did I keep feeling like there was something we'd missed?

***

"No further questions." Earl returned to his seat.

I glanced at the jury. A gray-haired Black woman nodded at me, and I smiled. The interrogation had gone exactly as we'd rehearsed it. My heart rate settled as Charlotte approached.

She studied the notes on her legal pad. "According to your testimony, Ms. Roma did a tarot reading for your husband that led you to the conclusion that she killed Madeleine. Is that correct?"

"Yes."

"And you also said that when you asked Ms. Roma if she murdered Madeleine, she said no. Why did you doubt her?"

"I just had a sixth sense that she was lying." It wasn't a lie. Duke was my extra sense.

Charlotte raised an eyebrow. "A sixth sense? Do you expect the jury to convict her based on your intuition?"

Earl stood. "Objection, Your Honor! Argumentative."

"Sustained."

"Let's talk about the Asian cookbook from The Cat's Meow. You deduced that Ms. Roma murdered Madeleine because it just happens to have a recipe for sushi rolls in it. Is that correct?"

"Objection." Earl slapped his hand on the table. "Leading the witness."

"Sustained. Ms. Sinclair, I'm warning you to watch how you phrase your questions."

"No need, Your Honor. I have no further questions." She smiled at me, then walked back toward her table.

As soon as the judge called a break, we left to pick up Duke. After we took our dog for a long walk, we ordered Chinese takeout and settled in to watch, *There's Something About Mary*. The moments of laughter eased the tension from the day. Right before dinner, Pete texted that the prosecution had rested its case, and the defense planned to call Sherry to the stand first thing tomorrow. We'd leave early. I wanted a front-row seat.

Even though we arrived half an hour early, the front row was filled, and we returned to our seats behind Clayton and Pete. I recognized several of the tenants in the audience, but there was no sign of Robert or Racheal. The room hummed in anticipation of Sherry's testimony.

The judge called the court to order and addressed Charlotte. "Counselor."

Charlotte stood. Today, she wore an elegant eggplant-colored blazer over a cream camisole and black pants. "The defense calls Sherry Roma to the stand."

As Sherry stepped forward, she smoothed the front of her black sheath dress. Her flaxen hair cascaded over her shoulders. Once she was sworn in, her lawyer approached the stand with a file folder clutched in one hand.

"Ms. Roma," Charlotte began, "please describe the nature of your relationship with Madeleine Collins."

"She was my landlady. I lease space in a strip center owned by the Collins."

"Thank you. And for the jury's benefit, please describe your business."

"I own a gift shop called The Cat's Meow."

Her attorney opened the file. "And where were you the evening of Saturday, May 12, 2018?"

"At home, with my cats." Sherry pursed her lips in a nervous smile while her eyes scanned the courtroom.

"Briefly describe your activities from when you left work until the next morning."

Sherry squirmed in her seat. "Um... I drove home, fed my cats, and then had dinner. After that..." She hesitated, her confidence wavering. Suddenly, she blurted out, "I didn't mean to kill Madeleine. I swear it was an accident."

The file full of papers tumbled out of Charlotte's hands as audible gasps resounded through the court.

Sherry seemed unable to stop herself. "I only wanted her to feel a smidgen of the misery she inflicted on everyone else," She continued, her voice rising. "She ran over my cat, Karma. She yelled and screamed at all the tenants. She belittled her husband. She was horrible!" Sherry cast a nervous glance toward Duncan as tears rolled down her cheeks.

People in the audience began to whisper, and the judge banged her gavel. "Order! Order in the court!"

Charlotte recovered her composure and said, "Your Honor, permission to approach the bench."

After a few minutes of hushed conversation passed, Charlotte returned to her seat. Judge Clark said, "Court is now in recess. We'll reconvene at 2:00 p.m. Mr. Beaufort and Ms. Sinclair, meet me in my chambers."

The bailiff said, "All rise."

I turned toward Brad, stunned. "What just happened?"

He shook his head. "I don't know, but that was an unexpected turn of events."

When the court reconvened, both attorneys delivered a brief closing statement. Judge Clark then provided the jury with instructions for their deliberations. The jury delivered its verdict in less than an hour.

After everyone settled back into the courtroom, Judge Clark addressed the assembly. "On the charge of first-degree murder, the jury finds Ms. Roma not guilty. The decision is unanimous."

A murmur rippled through the spectators as they digested the news.

"On the charge of involuntary manslaughter. The jury finds Ms. Roma guilty."

Sherry's shoulders slumped.

The judge continued, "The sentencing hearing will commence in courtroom number seven in fifteen minutes. Jurors, thank you for your service. Court is adjourned." Without another word, she exited toward her chambers.

Brad and I migrated to courtroom number seven and then sat in shock as Judge Clark read the sentence.

"Ms. Roma, considering your lack of prior criminal history, you are hereby sentenced to 500 hours of community service, to be completed within five years. I'm also assessing a $1,000 fine for the court's trouble. You are free to go. Ms. Sinclair will instruct you on the next steps."

On the way out of the courtroom, Sherry touched my arm. Her amber eyes were filled with remorse. "I'd like to buy you dinner at the Tipsy Tavern for the grief I've caused you."

Although her offer barely put a dent in the amends she owed me and others, I had lingering questions. Had she acted alone? Despite the lack of evidence of an accomplice, my gut said that was the piece I'd missed. Throughout the trial, she seemed to be protecting someone. But who? Maybe Duncan? Of course, I'd bring Duke along to confirm her answers.

Chapter 12

Since this was intended to be a girl's night out, Brad dropped us off and then headed into town to grab something to eat. Duke and I found Sherry at an outside table away from the other customers. As she sipped on a glass of bubbly, she perused the menu.

"Celebrating?" I asked as I took my seat.

"Well, hello there." She patted Duke's head. "Not really."

Duke yipped.

Sherry continued, "I just like their champagne."

Racheal hustled toward our table. "Hi, Liz. I'm surprised to see you here. I thought you'd head home right after the trial."

"Sherry offered to buy me dinner, so we decided to stay one more night."

Racheal gave Sherry a look that was hard to decipher. I wondered what that was about. "What can I get you to drink?" she asked.

I chose the most expensive wine on the menu, a Napa Valley cabernet, and ordered a can of the Session Squirrel dog beer for Duke.

"Any starters?"

"I'll take an order of the Tipsy Bites."

"Sherry?"

"Nothing for me."

"Be right back." Racheal turned and headed toward the bar.

I crossed my arms and glared at Sherry. "You got off light."

She gave a nervous laugh. "I'll be doing community service for the rest of my life."

I narrowed my eyes.

"I'm very sorry for what I put everyone through. It really was an accident."

No yip from Duke.

"Tell me the details of what happened that night. It's the least you can do."

She rubbed the edge of a cocktail napkin between her fingers. "You already heard most of it in the courtroom."

"I want to hear it again."

"I'd researched it. The amount of poisonous mushrooms I put in the sushi shouldn't have killed her—just made her really sick, like food poisoning."

"Go on." I nodded.

Sherry took a large gulp of champagne. "Halfway into her third roll, Madeleine clutched her stomach and ran for the bathroom. I wanted to give her privacy, so I didn't follow her. After about ten minutes, I checked on her." Sherry swallowed hard. "She was dead on the bathroom floor. I felt her pulse. Nothing." Her voice wavered as she dabbed her eyes with a napkin.

I had little sympathy. "So, why didn't you call for help?"

She hesitated. "It was awful. I panicked. I didn't know what to do."

That earned a yip from Duke. Did she not really know what to do, or was she glad Madeleine died?

My thoughts were interrupted when Racheal returned. She set the starter and my glass of wine on the table and then placed Duke's bowl of beer on the deck. He thumped a thank you with his tail.

"Have you decided what you want?"

I glanced at the menu. "I'll take the tenderloin, medium well, with the asparagus and a garden salad." I considered adding sauteed mushrooms but after the recent conversation decided against it.

"Dressing?"

"Ranch."

"Sherry, what will it be for you?"

She tapped her left palm on the table twice and then ordered the fish of the day, baked cod with pesto sauce, green beans, and cauliflower rice.

Racheal gave her a slight nod. "Got it. Another glass of champagne?"

"That'd be perfect."

Once Racheal disappeared inside, I asked, "So, what *did* you do?"

"Like I said, at first I panicked."

No yip from Duke.

"And then a plan started to form."

Duke yipped.

Sherry frowned. "Your dog's making that noise again. Does he need to pee?"

"I guess he does. Don't go anywhere." I wagged my finger at her before I turned to walk Duke to the grassy patch behind the parking lot. A quick break wouldn't hurt. I had all night to drag the truth out of her.

When I returned, Rachael was sitting in the seat beside Sherry, sipping a beer. The other patrons had left, and the patio was empty.

"It's slow inside, so Robert said I could join you guys." She lifted her mug. "Cheers."

We clinked glasses, and I picked up where Sherry and I had left off. "You were going to tell me what you did after you found her body."

Sherry opened her mouth, but before she could speak, Racheal groaned. "Seriously? You guys aren't talking about Madeleine's death, are you? C'mon, Liz, drop it. Sherry's already been convicted—it's old news." She took a long swig of beer and continued. "I rarely get a night off. Let's talk about something fun."

A glance passed between Sherry and Rachael, and I wondered if the palm tap had been some kind of signal.

No way was I going to drop it. I locked eyes with Sherry. "You had an accomplice didn't you?"

"No. Of course not."

Duke yipped.

"Liz, you're like a dog with a bone." Racheal patted Duke's head. "Has anyone seen that new movie *Truth or Dare*?"

"Not yet. I heard it wasn't very good," Sherry replied, eager to change the subject. I've been binge-watching episodes of *Forensic Files*. So good." She rubbed her hands together.

While they fell into casual chatter, my mind spun. I remembered the look Sherry gave Duncan in the courtroom. "It was Duncan. He helped you."

Sherry sighed. "I already told you. It was just me. No one else."

Duke yipped.

"What's the matter with your dog?" Racheal asked.

"I don't know. Maybe he wants another Session Squirrel?"

Duke made the same sound again.

Racheal looked back and forth between me and my dog. "Wait a minute..." She held up her mug. "This glass of wine sure tastes good."

Duke yipped again.

"Is your dog like a lie-detector or something?"

I shrugged.

"That's brilliant." When Sherry realized the implications, her face paled, and the corners of her lips dropped. She looked down at her lap and whispered. "It was Racheal."

"Sherry, shut up. You nimwit." She stomped her tiny foot on the wooden deck, and Duke whined.

No wonder it had taken an act of Congress to get Racheal to turn over her notebook to the cops.

The air was thick with tension when Robert arrived with our food. "Well, you ladies look like you're having fun. Can I get you anything else?"

"Just leave, Robert," Racheal growled.

He shrugged. "You don't have to tell me twice." Robert disappeared inside.

Sherry sighed. "We might as well tell her. Liz won't stop badgering us until she knows what happened that night."

Racheal stammered, "But... I don't want to go to jail."

"You didn't dump the body in the lake. Look at my sentence. You'll get something much lighter."

"Sherry's right. If you come clean about your part, you'll likely get something much less," I said.

Racheal shook her head. "I never said anything to Robert or Dad. I didn't want them to get into trouble if something went wrong. They're going to be so disappointed in me."

"I doubt it." Sherry chuckled awkwardly. "No one liked Madeleine. You'll be a local celebrity. People will flock to the bar just to get a glimpse of the Angry Elf."

"Fine. But you tell her. If you'd followed my advice—if you'd weighed the ingredients instead of measuring—Madeleine would still be alive, and we wouldn't be having this conversation." Racheal dressed her hamburger with lettuce, onions, and pickles from the side of her plate. "I told you. But did you listen? Of course not." She slapped the bun on top of the burger. "If you put flour or any other ingredient in a measuring cup, you'll get different amounts, but if you weigh it, you get the exact measurement."

"I was in a hurry."

"I was in a hurry," Racheal mocked her before she bit into her sandwich.

While I waited for Sherry to begin the recap of that fateful night, I carved a couple of bites of steak for Duke and set the feast in front of him. "Good boy."

Sherry leaned forward, "Racheal and I are true crime buffs. Every week, we watch *48 Hours* over drinks at each other's homes. The week after Madeleine killed my cat, the show was about a husband who'd poisoned his wife." She glanced at Racheal. "That's when we started talking about how we could make Madeleine suffer. We planned every detail, including what we'd do if something went wrong."

Racheal wiped ketchup from the side of her mouth. "Like Madeleine finding out about it, or God forbid, if Sherry killed her. When I got off work that night and saw the light on in the upstairs bedroom, my stomach dropped."

"I thought I was telling the story."

"Fine. Go ahead."

Sherry continued, "We had a code. If the upstairs light was on, Madeleine was dead, and Racheal would come over to implement project cover-up. I had a stash of supplies to erase any evidence that I'd bought with cash, just in case. If the downstairs study light was on, everything had gone according to plan."

Racheal interjected, "Of course that didn't happen."

Sherry glared at Racheal and then resumed, "Racheal snuck around the back, dressed in a black hoodie and sweatpants."

"I'd deliberately started a fight with Robert earlier in the week and was sleeping in the spare bedroom," Racheal added. "He never knew I was gone."

Sherry continued, "After she arrived, we hefted Madeleine's body into the trunk of my car and then cleaned the house until it was spotless, dumping everything into the trash."

Racheal picked up the thread. "We even picked a night before trash pick-up day so any evidence would be long gone before the body was discovered... except..." She paused for effect. "Sherry forgot to mention that the roses in the kitchen were from Madeleine until after she'd already taken the trash to the curb." She glared at Sherry. "Mistake number two. Oh, wait." She held up three fingers. "I left out confessing on the witness stand."

Sherry rolled her eyes. "Since the window to dump Madeleine's body into the lake was closing, we agreed that I'd toss the flowers on the back road where we'd chosen to dump the wet clothes."

Duke hadn't yipped once during the entire conversation. I turned toward Racheal. "So, are you going to share all of this with the cops, or do I need to?"

Racheal sighed. "I'll do it. Can we please just finish our dinner? Then I'll tell Dad and Robert. I promise to turn myself in tomorrow."

"Sure. Why not?" I replied.

***

About halfway into the drive back to Charleston, I received a text from Sherry that Racheal had been charged with obstruction of justice and fined $1,000, with no prison time or community service. After I shared the news with Brad, I said, "I keep turning it over in my mind. How did I miss Racheal's involvement?"

"Hon, you did everything you could. The truth eventually came out."

"Yeah, but it just doesn't feel like the punishment fit the crime." The second the words escaped my lips, I recalled Sherry's first reading: *truth and fairness will prevail, and karmic justice will be served.*

Was this karma? Did Madeleine's wrongdoings outweigh the consequences of a prank gone wrong? Then I remembered the meaning of the magician card: *someone may be trying to deceive you, and your goals may not be aligned with the highest good.*

After last night's big reveal, Sherry and Rachael had chatted about all the positive things that had occurred since their landlady's death. Not only was Duncan sober, he'd fostered stronger connections with all the tenants. He had even posted Sherry's bail, ensuring she could keep her business open prior to the trial. The center now hosted biannual fundraisers for brain cancer and alcohol addiction support.

"Do you believe in karma?" I asked Brad.

He tapped his fingers on the steering wheel as he thought. "I believe you should always try to do the right thing, and that you shouldn't mess with God's plans. If you call that karma, then yeah, I guess so. What about you?"

"I don't know. I'm still trying to wrap my head around everything. Last night, Rachael and Sherry listed all the good that had transpired since Madeleine's death."

"Well," Brad hesitated, then continued, "Some good things did come out of her death. I finally found some peace around the senselessness of my sister's drowning and the guilt I carried for not being able to save her."

"True." Brad hadn't had another nightmare. And I'd found peace around my bad childhood camping experience. We had even told Pete we'd return to Poinsett next spring, and I was looking forward to it.

But still, none of that justified Madeleine's death. Gunner had told me early on that there would always be at least one case that would haunt you.

This would be mine.

Acknowledgements

First and foremost, thank you, Lord, for the inspiration for the stories and the faith to carry them through. And a huge thank you to my family and friends, most especially my husband, Barry, who bears through the ups and downs with me.

A big shout-out to the real-life places and people who agreed to be a part of the story, fictionalized of course. Pecan Creek Grille is our favorite breakfast spot, and Tipsy Tavern is inspired by our go-to local pub, Finn MacCool's. Our amazing friends, Racheal and Robert, some of the best bartenders in Houston, lent their names and vibes to the story. Rachael's dad is not only a talented cook but also one of my beta readers. Michelle and DZ are my amazing hairstylists, and Joy's insurance agency is situated next to Pecan Creek Grille where Barry is fondly known as the biscuit boy for delivering treats to Maggie and Jemma.

To my fantastic beta readers, Tim Scanlan, Eileen Joyce Donovan, Liz Ivers, Laura Rader, David Trull, Mary Ellen Hendricks, and Sherry Hill—you are the best. Thank you, Jack McCloskey, for your feedback on the cover and the cover copy. Also, a shout-out to my editors, Tricia T. LaRochelle, Lone Star Literary, and Susan Fegraeus. Many thanks to my brilliant cover designer, Brandi Doane McCann, and the book trailer creator, Literary Titan.

And most importantly, a thank you to you, my readers. I couldn't exist without you. My mission is to deliver a good story to each of you while also benefiting a larger community. I donate a portion of the proceeds from the books to causes that help the homeless, both people and pets.

If you enjoyed the story, please spread the word, and leave a rating or review.

Keep turning the pages for Liz's recipes, a playlist, and a sample from the first book in the series, *Charleston Conundrum*.

Many thanks and happy reading!

All the best,

Stacy Wilder

www.storystacy.com

Maria's Asian Chicken Salad

Serves 4-6

Ingredients for the salad:

1 package coleslaw

1 cup salted sunflower seeds

1 cup toasted slivered almonds

2 green onions, chopped

2 packages Oriental ramen noodles (reserve the seasoning mix for the dressing)

1 cup shredded chicken (Maria uses precooked rotisserie chicken)

1 eleven ounce can of mandarin oranges (drained)

Preheat the oven to 350°F. Place the slivered almonds on a cookie sheet and roast for 5-8 minutes or until slightly brown. Add the above ingredients and the almonds to a salad bowl.

Ingredients for the dressing:

½ cup sugar

½ cup olive oil

1/3 cup white vinegar

2 packages Oriental seasoning mix

Whisk the above ingredients together and pour over the salad. Toss and serve.

Enjoy!

Ken's Macaroni Salad

Serves 8-10

(compliments of our friend, Ken Madliger, who says anyone who doesn't like it must leave! At times, I eat this for breakfast! Delicious.)

Ingredients:

16 ounce package of elbow macaroni small

3 jalapeno peppers

2 bunches green onions

4 celery sticks with leaves

1/3 cup parsley

1 teaspoon ground pepper

½ teaspoon salt

1 cup green olives with pimento (sliced)

4 hardboiled eggs

¼ cup olive oil

¾ cup real mayonnaise

Smoked paprika to taste

Hard boil 4 eggs, peel and slice. Set aside. Cook macaroni according to directions on package and drain. Chop celery, onion, jalapeno (core and remove seeds to reduce the heat), green olives, and parsley. Place drained pasta in a large mixing bowl and add the chopped ingredients. In a separate bowl or measuring cup, whisk together the olive oil, mayo, salt, and pepper. Pour the dressing into the salad and toss to combine. Add the sliced eggs and gently toss. Dust the top with smoked paprika. Cover and refrigerate until cold.

Enjoy!

Tipsy Bites

This recipe was influenced by Lady Racheal.

Ingredients:

Jumbo shrimp, peeled and deveined

Hickory bacon

Block of pepper jack cheese

Jalapeno

Your favorite barbecue sauce (Tipsy Tavern uses Sweet Baby Ray's Hickory & Brown Sugar)

Your favorite chipotle aioli

Preheat the oven to 425°F. Place a greased cooling rack on top of a cookie sheet. Butterfly the shrimp (slice down the middle). Thinly slice the jalapeno and cheese. Add a slice of jalapeno and cheese to the middle of the shrimp and fully wrap in bacon. Thread shrimp onto metal skewers to make it easier to flip. Place the full skewers on top of the rack. Bake for 20 minutes, flipping shrimp halfway through. Brush one side of the shrimp with barbecue sauce and cook for five more minutes, then flip and repeat. Serve the shrimp with a side of chipotle aioli for dipping.

Enjoy!

S'mores Bars

Makes 16 bars

Ingredients:

½ cup unsalted butter (softened)

¾ cup light brown sugar

1 large egg

1 teaspoon vanilla extract

1 cup all-purpose flour

1 cup graham cracker crumbs

½ teaspoon baking powder

¼ teaspoon salt

1 cup semi-sweet chocolate chips

1 heaping cup store bought marshmallow crème

Preheat oven to 350°F. Grease an 8 inch square baking pan on all sides. In a large bowl, cream together the butter and brown sugar. Add the egg and vanilla extract and mix until combined. In a separate bowl, whisk together the flour, graham cracker crumbs, baking powder, and salt. Pour the flour mixture into the large bowl and beat on medium speed until combined. Spread two-thirds of the dough into the pan. Then spread the marshmallow crème on top. Evenly sprinkle the chocolate chips on top of the crème. Form the remaining dough into 8-10 round balls and then flatten. Layer the flattened dough in intervals on top of the cholate chips, leaving some of the marshmallow/chocolate chip areas exposed. Bake for 25-30 minutes, until the top is lightly browned. Remove from oven and allow the bars to cool. Once cooled, cut into squares.

Enjoy!

A Camping Conundrum Playlist

1. "Love Shack," The B-52's

2. "These Boots Are Made for Walkin'," Nancy Sinatra

3. "Crazy," Patsy Cline

4. "Hit Me with Your Best Shot," Pat Benatar

5. "I Will Survive," Gloria Gaynor

6. "The Lady Is a Tramp," Ella Fitzgerald

7. "My Favorite Things," Julie Andrews

8. "Brown Eyed Girl," Van Morrison

9. "The House of the Rising Sun," The Animals

10. "Ring of Fire," Johnny Cash

11. "Here Comes the Sun," The Beatles

12. "Blowin' in the Wind," Bob Dylan

13. "Moondance," Van Morrison

14. "Danger Zone," Kenny Loggins

15. "Building a Mystery," Sarah McLachlan

16. Bonus – "A Bar Song (Tipsy)," Shaboozey

A Sample from Charleston Conundrum

L iz stretched the packing tape over the last box. The movers were due to arrive any minute. Referring to the yellow legal pad, she double-checked her list.

"Stock options cashed—check. Divorce papers finalized with lying, cheating bastard of an ex-husband—check. Atlanta house sold—check. Closed on townhouse in Charleston —check. Signed up for classes to obtain PI license—check." A tear escaped from the corner of her eye. "Damn it, Sawyer," she swore at her ex.

She chewed on the end of her pen and looked around the boxed-up space they once called home. The hardwood floors lovingly restored. The walls painted a soft cream. They'd spent hours picking out the perfect shade. The upstairs bedrooms would never be filled with the children they both had so desperately wanted. Thirty-one, and divorced. Not the life she'd imagined a few years ago when she believed in their love. His betrayal still stung. Her blue eyes misted. "No more tears." She brushed off her hands in an attempt to dismiss any lingering memories.

A wet nose nudged her leg. "Hey, Duke." The puppy was a last-minute addition to the trip. One of her co-workers at Coca-Cola couldn't keep him. At six months, he was already fifty pounds of boundless energy. Who could resist an adorable black Lab puppy?

"Dog crate ready for road trip to Charleston—check."

Her cell phone buzzed, and she recognized the number. "Hi, Mom."

"Hi, hon. You all packed?"

"Yup."

"Are you sure you want to go? Why don't you come to Florida and spend a few months with Dad and me?"

Liz swallowed hard as tears threatened once again. "Too late. Movers will be here any minute. I'll call you when I get there."

Her parents were convinced she was having a nervous breakdown after the divorce. They couldn't believe she quit her cush job, sold the house, and was moving to Charleston, South Carolina.

"Suck it up," she muttered. Then she perched her petite frame on the built-in window seat and watched for the moving van. She didn't think it was possible to fall in love with a place, but Charleston gave her hope she hadn't felt in a long while. Time for a fresh start. As she tucked a stray blonde hair behind her ear, she recalled the moment she decided to move.

Walking down East Bay, her whole life upended, a soft salty breeze offered some relief from the sweltering heat. She could feel Charleston seeping into her skin. It was as if nothing mattered, and everything mattered all in the same breath. The slight scent of hay, and horse sweat coming from a nearby carriage beckoned her to rest her feet and take a ride. Facing a pending divorce and a career that kept her busy, yet not satisfied, she was not looking forward to returning to Atlanta. This place enchanted her. Homes, hundreds of years old, were painted the colors of Crayola crayons. The never-ending Southern porches were dotted with wooden swings and wicker rockers. The azalea and camellia bushes were in full bloom and the scent of jasmine collided with the salt air. The clip-clop rhythm of horses' hooves against the weathered street left her longing for a more natural rhythm in her own life. Every one of her senses was engaged; the backs of her thighs sticky with sweat against the hard brown leather carriage seat; the smell of salt, hay, and perspiration; the Caribbean green, periwinkle blue, carnation pink of the houses; the taste of salt as she licked her dry lips; the musical sound of birds singing. She sighed. It had been a long time since she had felt this alive. Perhaps it was time for a permanent change of scenery.

The sound of the moving van approaching her driveway popped her back to the present. Planting a kiss on top of Duke's head, she said, "Charleston, here we come!"

www.ingramcontent.com/pod-product-compliance
Lightning Source LLC
Chambersburg PA
CBHW031517010826
48973CB00013B/2682